CHANGING
WAYS
Bruce Ario 2020

"I still have much up my sleeve."
— Ahmed Mostafa

"Make a joyful noise unto the Lord"   Psalm 100

Dedicated to
Cyndy

The white stucco walls of the first floor master bedroom in the Tudor home seemed unusually white as Bill McCutcheon arose his first day as inaugurate judge in the Manhattan Mental Health Court.` Bill focused on the yellow oak beams in the ceiling for a moment, then, he was ready. He neatly made the king-sized bed with hospital corners for the blanket and sheet and covered them with the tan comforter which had kept him warm in the 68 degree temperature room. He went to the adjacent bathroom. He posed in the mirror over the sink, lathered up and shaved as he gave himself tough guy glances. He opened the glass shower door and then showered for five minutes and used a salon shampoo which left his full head of brown hair looking sexy. He went back to the sink and brushed his teeth and realized his moustache was long. He dug out his trimmer. He opened the medicine cabinet and went through his regimen of vitamins. He splashed on a little aftershave, and walked back out to the bedroom and over to the closet. He selected his Tommy Hilfiger white shirt, his Calvin Klein black trousers, and his Ralph Lauren red tie. He looked at his Bostonian black wingtips and winced. He would have to get them polished at the shoeshine on the way. When he was all dressed, he left the bedroom, shut the door, and went to the base of the main stairway.

"Sara?" he called up the stairs.
No answer.
"Sara?"
"Whhhaaattt?" Sara, Bill's only child, and live-at-home 22-year-old, shrieked back.
"Sara, it's the big day."

"I'm not in the mood."

Bill walked up the golden carpeted staircase, past the family portrait that included his separated wife, Dorothy, past the leaded glass window that showed the sun in the East, and up to the door of Sara's bedroom.

He knocked.
"Sara? Sara. Can't you be a little more enthused?"
"About what?"
"Sara? Don't you remember it's my first day as a judge?"
Sara opened the bedroom door.
"You seem to want to make such a big deal out of nothing."

Sara's unruly, red hair hung over her eyes. She wore a giant green White Plains High School sweatshirt, orange jogging pants, and gray wool socks. Behind her lie a room in disarray – unmade bed, TV blaring, computer monitor on, books and papers strewn all over, and used dishes, glasses, and food containers everywhere.

"Sara. I was hoping you'd be a little excited."
"Oh right. I'm supposed to be the mentally challenged girl who's honored that her father cares so much for her that he's become a judge in the all new Manhattan Mental Health Court. Do you want me to bow?"
"Sara, I won't tolerate backtalk."

Sara slammed the door.

Bill, raising his voice, said, "Sara, I'm leaving, and I hope you make it in to work today or there'll be consequences."

Bill descended the stairs and walked into an elongated and cheerful kitchen that had a center island and a table and two chairs. The window showed a large backyard with a deck and all the furnishings. The smell of coffee already permeated the air; the timer always worked. He went to the refrigerator, pulled out a banana, orange, and a quart of vanilla yogurt, then threw them in the blender for a minute. He poured the smoothie into a large glass and downed it in half a minute. He emptied the coffee pot into his travel mug.

At the door of the house on Broadway in White Plains, NY, lie the New York Times. He would read it as he rode the Metro North Train to Williams Bridge, then he would take a short walk over to the Gun Hill Road stop on the 5 line subway, and ride to the Brooklyn Bridge/City Hall stop. He would then walk to the court building at 100 Centre St. But Bill had to struggle today to concentrate on the purview of the new job; truthfully the type of interaction he had just had with Sara was becoming way too typical. It was a great source of mental pain. Nonetheless, he knew his job came first.

"Hello, I need to speak to Lisa Yackel."
"Sara McCutcheon."
"Lisa, this is Sara. I won't be coming into work today."
"Yes, I know I can't take off work for mental health problems. That isn't what it is. I…I sprained my… foot."
"Suu..rre. I'll bring a note from the doctor when I come in tomorrow."

Sara went back to her bedroom, cued up an Earthday record, and put on her headphones.

Bill arrived at the court building. There was a shoe shine worker in the lobby.

"Please give them a once over," said Bill.
"How's your day going so far?" asked the young worker.
"Besides my daughter?"
"I've got one too."
"My daughter is considerably older and more trouble I'm sure."

Then Bill went up to the 15th floor. He was still somewhat spry on his feet at 57 years old, and his brown hair had just a little gray around the temples. He carried a briefcase which held the Times, his empty travel mug, and a bag of peanuts: his lunch.

Molly was right there at the elevator when it opened at 7:30 sharp, Wednesday, March 16, 2011.

"Judge McCutcheon."
"Oh, no,Molly. Don't start getting formal after all these years."

Molly had been Bill's admin assistant for nearly 20 years, and one of the few requests made by Bill when he was designated as judge is that Molly follow him in her support role. Molly, who was about Bill's age, wore her gray hair in a bun and a conservative mid-calf dress by Jones. Her shoes were flats, and she wore stockings, something that the younger set had largely left by the wayside.

"Bill, then. Yes. Let me show you where they have you located."

She led Bill down a marbled hallway attractively lined with abstract art, but Bill noticed there were no windows.

"I hope I have at least one window, Molly," said Bill half-joking, half-hoping.

"You, my dear, have a corner room with four windows."

Molly opened the door to his chambers with grand gesture. The chambers had numerous shelves that were stocked with countless court reporters, New York and federal books of statutes, several varieties of dictionaries, miscellaneous reference books, and a collection of non-fiction books about mental illness. He had a PC on his desk as well as a picture of Sara at her high school graduation. The floor was red shag carpet and the walls were mostly mahogany, but what really grabbed Bill were the windows.

"Molly, I have got a view!" Bill looked out on Wall Street, lower Manhattan, and the Atlantic Ocean.

"Don't get too distracted Bill. Your first meeting is in 15 minutes."

With that, Molly closed the door and left Bill to more carefully survey his new surroundings. He sat down and leaned back in his immense black leather chair, folded his hands together, and then allowed himself a stretch and a smile. *Even Sara won't ruin this moment.*

"Bain, I need a note." Sara was talking to her boyfriend on the phone.

"A note from a doctor that says I have a sprained ankle."

"If I want an official note it will cost me how much?"

" Bain, I'd have to work for a week to earn that. But I'll tell you what. Stop by my old man's house with the note before 3:00 today, and I'll do you one of my little favors. Groovy?"

Sara had her note, and Bain out the door by 4:00, a half hour before her father would come home. The note was from a doctor, who cheated on those kinds of things, and it even listed a name to call for verification if Sara's boss was inclined to check. Sara took an ace bandage from the linen closet and wrapped up her foot and ankle. Then she practiced limping down the hallway back to her room. When Bill came home she was lying down in her bed.

"Is that you Bill?" called Sara from her room.

"Dad. I'm your dad. Not Bill. And why are you home?" asked the judge as he walked up the stairs.

"Father, I fell down the stairs on my way to work. I sprained my ankle. The doctor said it isn't broke though."

"You had to go to a doctor? Oh, hon' I'm so sorry."

"Medical assistance will pay for it."

"I thought you lost your coverage when you moved from the Washington Lodge back home."

"No. No Bil... I mean Dad. I worked it out." Sara was lying.

"Well O.K., but if you get a bill, I'll pay for it. I don't want to see you get socked for a medical bill when you've got so little income."

"Don't worry. If I need money, I'll let you know. Now could you please leave? My show is coming on." She looked over at the TV.

"I'll call you for dinner in an hour, Sara," said Bill.

He walked down the stairs and into the kitchen.

"Let's see. I think we'll have spaghetti."

In lower Manhattan, in Battery Park, a young Korean-American man ran past a senior woman, grabbed her purse out of her hands, and sprinted. She screamed and caught the attention of a cop. The young cop was quicker than the thief and ran down the Asian who didn't resist. The cop frisked the man over his black leather jacket which had the insignia "On the Road to Hell". The man still gripped the purse.

"You're going to jail for a while my friend."
The young man looked shocked. All he said was, "Why?"
"You have someone else's money here pal." The cop gritted his teeth, and he snarled his words as he grabbed the purse.
"No. It's my money," the young man said almost timidly.
The police officer scoffed, "Oh, smart aleck, hey?"

The two men were drawing a crowd.

The Korean asked, "Who are you?"
The cop was surprised at that one. "A New York City police officer."
"No. I don't believe you. I think you're the Mafia. You've come to kill me. Just do it. Get it over with."

Then it began to register with the officer. He had studied this in training. What he had was a psychotic man unless he was a very good faker. The officer was aware of the bystanders and knew he must do something.

"Buddy, I think you're off your rocker. Come with me. I'm taking you to the hospital."

The people who had been watching it all looked at the purse in the officer's hand.

"What about the purse?" someone shouted.

"I'm giving it back to its owner," said the cop handing it over to the elderly woman. "I'll need no evidence. There is no crime."

Shock registered on the faces of several in the crowd. Relief came over the faces on others.

One guy said to a man next to him, "Just act crazy and you can do just about anything under the sun."

A middle-aged woman who looked like she might have been a librarian or something similar said, "Shame on you two. Can't you see that young man was very sick?"

The first guy said, "You'd feel differently if he had grabbed your purse, lady."

"I'd consider it an inconvenience, but I wouldn't want him to go to jail. He needs help."

"It's you do-gooders why we have a problem," said the second man, puffing on a cigar.

Bill reached for a box of noodles in the cupboard and turned on a flame below a pot of water while tossing in the noodles. He took a pound of frozen ground beef from the freezer and put it in the microwave to thaw. Then, when the hamburger meat was thawed, he broke off chunks and threw them onto a fry pan. He opened a can of tomato paste and poured it over the meat. He diced up some onions and threw them in. By that time, the noodles were cooked. He strained them and dumped them in a bowl. He poured the meat sauce over the noodles. Next, he took a bag of Romaine lettuce, shook out the leaves into a strainer running water over them, and then onto two salad plates. For himself, he used Italian dressing; for Sara, he used Thousand Island. He poured himself a glass of Burgundy and Sara, a glass of milk.

"Saaarrraaa. Time to eeeaaattt." Bill shouted.

"I'm not hungry," yelled down his daughter.

"Sara, I made spaghetti for you," he said, almost subdued. Bill was getting tired of screaming up the stairs.

"I'm going out for pizza with Bain."

At that, Bill immediately climbed the staircase to Sara's room.

"Sara, you're not going out tonight if you didn't go to work today."

"My ankle is feeling better."

"Well, I'm glad to hear that, but I don't care too much for that Bain boy."

"Bill, I'm 22 years old and I don't think you have a right to tell me how to choose my friends."

"When you're living under my roof, I have lots of rights to tell you lots of things."

"Then I'll move back into the Washington Lodge."

"Will they have you in the Lodge?"

The next morning after Bill had left for court, Sara was on the phone to Lisa, the coordinator of Washington Lodge.

"Lisa, I want to come back to Washington Lodge."

"What's up?"

"I need the structure of a Lodge."

"Are you just saying that to make it sound good?"

"I realize I've got some things I need to work on."

"Sara, cut the crap."

"What?"

"I won't repeat it."

"O.K. O.K. Bill's putting pressure on me."

"Bill? You mean your father?"

"Yeah. He's coming down hard."

"Is there a reason why he should be?"

"Hey. Are you going to let me back in the Lodge or not?"

"Sara, you know how these things work. The Lodge clients must vote on it."

"Can I come to the vote?"

"Tomorrow at nine."

Bill was at work, Day 2, and meeting with his mental health court staff.

"So, the theory, Judge McCutcheon..."
"It's 'Bill'. Everyone here is on a first name basis."
"O.K. So the theory is, Bill, that the mental health court will be a win for a lot of people."

The 40ish paralegal was brought in from Idaho where they had instituted a mental health court a decade ago. "First, and most importantly, it's the best option for the offenders. Of course, they have to have a diagnosed serious mental illness to the degree that they had no criminal intent in their actions. That is, they had a major block sufficient to render them unable to know right from wrong or control their impulses. By working them through their issues in mental health court they get a chance to really change themselves and get on the road to recovery.

"The next benefactor is society. There has not been a conclusive study made yet, but the savings over a year have a potential to be significant between what mental health court costs and what criminal court and jail costs.

"Thirdly, it is the just thing to do. How can you really punish mental illness? It's no one's fault. Certainly, it's not the fault of the offenders. They didn't ask to have the illness..."

Bill had a flash where he thought some of the people with mental illness could take more important steps to alleviate their illness. But maybe they needed forgiveness. He thought of Sara.

"Sara, didn't your Wellness Counselor at the Washington Lodge tell you about getting regular exercise?"

Bill McCutcheon was on the phone when his daughter was an 18-year-old in 2008 and lived at the Washington Lodge on Long Island. The Washington Lodge was a program based on the Fairweather Model which was developed by George Fairweather in the 1960's. The program had had huge successes where it was employed. The pivotal idea was that people with mental illness could recover through peer support. Clients lived in a Lodge, a home in the community, and they worked together in a business to cover expenses. Sara had told her father what she had for dinner – hamburger, fries and soda.

"Well usually I eat with the others, but tonight I'm just doing my own thing."
"Don't the others object?"
"They'll probably fine me, but that's O.K."
"You have to try to work with the others, Sara."
"Dad, I've got to go."

Bill had then gotten on the phone with Lisa Yackel, the staff worker for the Washington Lodge.

"Lisa, this is Sara's father."
"Yes, Mr. McCutcheon, what can I do for you?"
"Lisa, how is Sara doing in the program?"
"Did you try asking her?"
"Well…I guess I was wanting to know your viewpoint."
"Mr. McCutcheon, I usually don't discuss the clients behind their backs."
"Oh, what I mean is I think she needs help."

"Mr. McCutcheon, I'm sorry to cut you off, but I have a meeting I'm needing to get to."

"Why yes. Thank you, Lisa. Will I be talking to you again?"

"Good byyee."

2

On the subway ride home after his second full day as a judge, Bill was reading a book about dual-dependency. It was relevant to the situation with Sara. She was MI-CD – Mentally Ill and Chemically Dependent. She hadn't accepted that she was. She wanted freedom to do whatever she wanted, but Bill knew alcohol was a negative factor.

> *So, you see, the mental health field claims that people drink or use illicit drugs to alleviate their symptoms of mental illness. The substance abuse field says that people are mentally ill as a result of their use of alcohol and/or drugs.*
> *Can you have it both ways? I think so. As a MD and psychiatrist who is also a diagnosed schizophrenic and who is personally in recovery from alcohol, I look at the dual nature of the illness.*
> *I can't say I became crazy, then drank. Nor can I say I drank, then became crazy. They both seemed to happen at about the same time in my life which was in my early 20's. It is entirely unclear to me that one caused the other. They seemed to go hand-in-hand if you will.*
> *I am able to say they both exasperated each other...*

Bill thought, oh yes. That's certainly true for Sara. Bill read a little further,

> *...but I strive to keep them as separate illnesses in my mind despite the overlap in symptoms. For my schizophrenia I take medications and see a therapist. For my alcoholism I go to AA. Now I know it is a tradition in AA to remain anonymous at the level of press, but...*

Bill put the book back down. He asked himself, why does he break the tradition? I thought AA believed in closed-lips. Doesn't anyone have privacy anymore? Any sense of shame? Any sense of a greater good?

It was Friday, and Sara was at the Washington Lodge begging to get back in. When she left the Lodge two years ago to go back home, she continued her job as a janitor with the agency which was allowed, but now Sara wanted back in the Lodge. "I can't take Bill anymore," she said to herself.

"Are you guys gonna let me back in the Lodge or not?" Sara was blunt.

"Sara, somebody has to make a motion. Then we have discussion. Then we get to a vote."

Millie, the Lodge Chairman, was all about rules. She felt it was how the Lodge functioned.

"Can I move that I be let back in?" Sara pushed the envelope.

"No Sara. You're not a member as of right now. You can only state your case in discussion." Millie was firm.

"I suppose I move to let Sara back in Washington Lodge." Jim, a sandy-haired, slender, young man had always been a friend to Sara. He was in the Lodge when Sara previously resided there.

"We need a second to the motion." Millie stated the rule per usual.

"I second," said Liz, a relative newcomer in the Lodge. She looked and acted like she was up for just about anything. She had multi-colored hair and multiple piercings.

"We'll now have discussion. Sara, you can state your case."

Millie placed both her hands on the table and looked down her nose.

Sara swallowed deep and began, "I want to say. Well. I guess I'm going through some tough times. I need the Lodge. I need you guys."

"I don't know if you mean it, Sara."

Millie looked around the table where the four others and Sara sat. The dining room was adjacent to a slightly larger living room. Two large canvas paintings hung in the Lodge, both in the next room, were bucolic scenes. The walls were painted a light blue. The window in the dining room was a large bay window. Outside, a neighbor was coming out of his house and down the walk. The physical tone of the Lodge was that of a family setting.

"Sara, can you promise that you'll pull your weight?"

Liz threw out the question to pin Sara down because even she wasn't sure about Sara.

Sara looked over at one of the paintings, the one with a farmer in the field. It made her feel like she was home because her grandfather had been a farmer.

"I always have," said Sara.

"We all know that's not true, Sara," interjected Millie. "You were known to miss Lodge meetings, miss group meals, and get sick a whole lot at work."

"I didn't miss so many meetings. I was just late. The reason I didn't eat with you guys is because I have food allergies. I can't help it if I really get sick."

Sara looked around the table. She knew Millie would vote against her, but she was sure Jim would vote for her and probably Liz. Of the two remaining Lodge members, Ken and Joan, Sara would have to win one of them over.

"Didn't I add some life to the Lodge when I was here?"

Sara was stating her case in a straight-forward manner, putting all her cards on the table.

"I was only here for the last year of your three year stay," said Ken, "but, yes you were fun to be around ..."

Sara immediately seized that moment as a victory.

"...when you weren't sulking..."

Sara's jaw dropped.

"...but you were the life of the Lodge..."

Sara brightened.

"...most of the time."

I have him, thought Sara.

"O.K. Let's get on with it," Millie said in her quasi-authoritarian manner. "All those in favor of admitting Sara back into the Lodge signal by raising your right hand."

Jim's hand shot up, then Liz's. There was an awkward silence. Millie looked as if she was about to say something when Sara stared over at Ken seemingly drawing his right hand out of his lap and into the air. It was Friday and Sara was in.

Bill read on as he rode the train home on the preceding day of Sara's ordeal, Thursday.

> ...I feel a sense of urgency because there is much need out there and AA has helped me so much that I cannot be silent...

Bill thought, I'm trying to make Sara silent. Perhaps I'm reading the wrong book. But he read on.

> ....I have found that the intimacy of therapy can coexist with the openness of an AA meeting...

Bill pondered, Sara's got the group experience of a Lodge. Maybe she needs the one-on-one with someone.

> After much soul searching and many different experiences, I have determined that balance in recovery is essential.

Sara balanced? Well, when she was a little girl...

"Daddy, I need to bring something to Show-n-Tell for school tomorrow."

"Well Sara, you've got to figure out why you want to bring something first."

"Because Miss Ginger asked me to."

"Well that's a good reason, but why else?"

"Because I want to share."

"Why do you want to share?"

"I don't know."

"Is it because you like the others?"

"Yeah."

"What do you think they'd like you to show them?"

"Something fun."

"Could you show them your ukulele?"

"Yes. I want to."

"Saaarrraaa?"

Bill had just come through the front door of their home on Thursday evening, a day before Sara was to approach the Lodge.

"I'm in my room, Bill."

Bill bit his tongue deciding not to push her on her selection of names for him. Tomorrow was Friday, the end of the judge's first work week. Two days after that it would be Sunday. Bill and Sara almost never missed a Sunday meal together. The tradition had been set in Sara's infancy.

"Sara," Bill called up the stairs. "What time are we getting together on Sunday?"

"Oh boy, Bill. I hadn't thought about it yet. You know…well I guess you don't know, I'm going to try to get back to the Washington Lodge tomorrow. Could we skip it this time?"

Bill walked upstairs to just outside Sara's door.

In a calm and measured tone of voice he said, "Sara, I know you've had it rough lately…"

"Yeah, for about the last five years."

"…but I think it's a dangerous precedent if we don't have our Sunday dinner together."

"Oh Gawd."

"Sara, you're my daughter. I don't ask much of you, but I do ask this much – that you honor our Sunday dinners."

"O.K. All right. But it has to be on these terms: that the conversation is open. You can't muzzle me, Bill. I will be heard."

3

The McCutcheon's – Bill, Dorothy, and Sara – came through the front door of their Tudor home on Broadway. It was a Sunday in January in 2000.

"This talk about the Millennium stuff should be over by now."

Dorothy took off her coat and boots.

"Simmons ought to be preaching new material. It's been a couple of weeks."

She helped the 10-year-old, Sara, off with her coat.

"Sometimes I feel Simmons just isn't with it. He's stuck in the last century."

"It's only been a couple of weeks into the 21st century," said Bill also taking off his coat. "Besides what else is there to talk about?"

They hung their coats in the closet by the door. Then Dorothy went into the kitchen to prepare dinner. Bill turned on the playoff football game, the St. Louis Rams and the Minnesota Vikings. Sara went out into the center of the living room. She sat in the blue wing-back chair with her color crayons and coloring book.

"Keep your feet off the ottoman, Sara," said Bill as he kept both eyes on the game.

"But that's what it's for," replied Sara.

"No. It's for looks."

In a short hour, Dorothy had dinner on the table in the dining room.

They sat down to eat. The TV was still on.

"Bill, do we have to have the game on? Wouldn't it be nice if we could talk sometimes?"

Dorothy would try, but it was always a losing affair.
"Honey, it's a big game."
"Aren't they all big, Bill?"
"Honey?"
"It's O.K. Sara and I will talk."

They moved their chairs facing each other.

"Sara, what did you learn about in Sunday School?"

Bill took his plate, grabbed a TV tray, and went into the living room.

"We talked about Jesus in the temple talking to the elders. Mary and Joseph couldn't find him, but there he was."
"What'd you think about that, Sara?"
"Is that like people Grandpa's and Grandma's age?"

When Judge McCutcheon arrived at court at 7:30 on Monday, he was told by Molly that the first defendant would go before him at 9:00. Before that he would be meeting with the prosecutor and the defense attorney who would lay out the strategy.

Scott Jensen was a veteran prosecutor, one who McCutcheon was familiar with from the days when they had practiced law at the Federal District Court for Southern New York. The two had been on opposing sides several times, but were friendly. He was dressed in a conservative gray suit and red tie.

Marie Gonzalez was a young attorney just out of Harvard Law School who was working pro bono in the mental health court, at least partly, to have her student loans forgiven. She wore a turquoise Aztec maxi dress.

They came into the chambers together.

"Scott, good to see you. Marie, nice to meet you."

The judge shook both their hands.

Jensen spoke, "Bill, it's great to see you in this position. I understand the mental health court is somewhat of an experiment. What with the population of persons with mental illness in our jails, this just may be the ticket. The clients should be quite grateful that they can bypass criminal court."

Gonzalez quickly chimed in, "Mental illness is not a choice. We shouldn't be criminalizing it in the first place."

The two attorneys locked eyes for a second, but McCutcheon stepped in and said, "We all three know that it's not a free ride for the defendants, but it does provide an alternative to more punitive measures. The idea is to create law abiding citizens."

McCutcheon pulled out two chairs at a table and took his seat behind his desk.

"So, brief me on the first defendant in Manhattan Mental Health Court."

Jensen started, "His name is Louis Chang. He's a naturalized citizen, single, born in South Korea, came here to school, and stayed. He had a job as a computer software designer which he lost in the 2008 Recession. He had trouble getting back on his feet. He had sporadic contact with the mental health system. He worked intermittently at temp jobs but hadn't worked for over a year when he was apprehended last week after he stole a woman's purse. He was observed for 24 hours at Bellevue Hospital in their psych ward. A mental health case manager was assigned from the Department of Health and Mental Hygiene. He was transferred to Rikers Island for the weekend. He is out in the lobby now."

"Ms. Gonzalez?"

"He should have never been brought to Rikers. He showed classic signs of schizophrenia with hallucinations and voices. He was on an anti-psychotic several years ago, but went off it because he didn't feel he had a problem."

"Is he on medication now?"

"Yes," said Gonzalez. "We've also made some treatment plans. His case worker, Lenny Barnes has the details."

"Where's Mr. Barnes?"

"Out in the lobby with Chang. I think it's best not to leave Louis on his own."

"I'll have my admin, Molly, watch Chang," said McCutcheon. Over the intercom the judge told Molly to summon in Barnes and to keep her eye on the defendant.

"Is Chang safe with Molly?" asked Jensen.

"She's good. She'll put him at ease."

In the lobby, Molly approached Chang. "I'm sure everything will work out."

In a minute, Barnes, the case manager was in the chambers. He was an aging man, probably close to retirement. He wore a baggy sweater and khaki pants.

"Mr. Barnes, can you lay out the treatment plan for our client?"

"Let's see." He fumbled with some paperwork. "Give me…ah, here we go. Louis will need to be med compliant and will see a psychiatrist every two weeks for a year, then, uh, once a month. He must attend AA meetings twice a week. He must, um, see a therapist once a week. And he must, *cough*, actively seek employment for at least 10 hours a week. Of course, he also must not have any offenses. For two years that is."

They talked another five minutes.

"O.K. Very good. Let's go to court."

The judge led the way out of the chambers, gathered Chang, and they all walked down the hall to the courtroom. The judge took his seat at the bench. The others sat at a table in front of him.

"Will the defendant, Louis Chang, please rise."

Together they went over the plan that had been laid out in the chambers.

"Mr. Chang? Do you think you're ready and able to follow this plan?"

"Yes, your honor."

"Mr. Chang, you have the good fortune to be our first client to pass through Manhattan Mental Health Court. I hope you can live up to your word."

"You honor, I intend to be worthy of your trust."

About noon, Sara was on the phone.

"Lisa, I need someone to come here and pick up me and my stuff."

"You want someone to drive from Long Island to White Plains to get you? That's 30 miles."

"I'll pay you."

"You bet you will."

"Bain, you in the mood?"

Sara looked over at Bain who was dressed in all black with chains around his neck and wrists.

"What?"
"You know."
"How much do you need?"
"A hundred."
"You better treat me real nice."

In the van on the way to Long Island, Sara asked Lisa, "I suppose I got to go to work today."
"I suppose you do."
"Isn't it a little late? I mean the shift started two hours ago."
"Look Sara. Do you want to be in the Lodge or not?"
"O.K. O.K. I just asked."
Lisa pulled the van up in front of H. Lee Dennison COUNTY Executive BUILDING IN SUFFOLK COUNTY.

"All right Sara. You know the drill."
"What about my stuff?"

"Sara, pick up your stuff off the dining room table. I'm trying to get dinner on it."
It was Sunday at the McCutcheon's home. Dorothy was telling the eight-year-old to gather her school books and make room for the chicken dinner. Sara dutifully complied.

"Bill, do we have to have the TV on?"
"Honey, it's a big game."
"What?"
"The Yankees and the White Sox."
"I swear Bill. Your sports are going to come between us."

Bill put his index finger up to his lips, and gestured over at Sara. Dorothy shrugged her shoulders. The parents sometimes thought Sara was oblivious to their quarreling, but the sudden look of hurt on Sara's face was too apparent to be passed over.

"Sara, what's wrong honey?" asked Dorothy.

Sara's eyes got big, then she looked down and said, "You and Daddy are always fighting."

Bill took a deep breath. "Sara, I'm sorry. I'll turn off the game."

"No, Daddy. I know you like to watch baseball. I don't want you to miss the game for me."

"Well what then?" asked Dorothy.

"Mommy, we can talk while Daddy watches the game."

"Then we're not eating together as a family."

Dorothy put both hands on her hips and looked over at Bill.

"You two have girl talk and I'll watch baseball. Dorothy, Sara is O.K. with that."

"Girl talk?" scoffed Dorothy. "Sounds so trivial."

"I'm not saying that at all," said Bill.

"You two are females and you should have things to share."

"Bill, why do I feel like you're just trying to avoid your responsibilities?"

"Honey, you are really twisting things around."

"Please. Stop fighting. It's all because of me." Sara looked up at them and tried to smile.

"No honey. It's not because of you."

Dorothy bent over and looked in Sara's eyes. Then she stood up and looked at Bill. Her look said, *"Can't you see what you've done."*

Then Sara saved the day when she said, "Let's all watch the game."

"That's my little girl," beamed Bill.

Several weeks into his job as judge, one morning on the subway, Bill put the Times down and looked around the car. He thought there were about 40 people. He had read that 1 in 10 people have a diagnosable mental illness so that means about four people in this car have the illness. He was above trying to figure out which ones they were. It was an impossible task anyway. Mental illness was the invisible disease. There really was no way of knowing for sure without asking, and he couldn't do that. Just as well he thought. No one really needs to know. What was really in the back of Bill's mind was the question of what would he do if people found out that he, now a judge, had been in a mental health facility as a youth? Had society come far enough to allow this? He wasn't breaking any laws. He had both feet in reality at this point in his life. Nonetheless, the feeling that he might be deemed by society to be less than fit to be a judge gnawed at him. After all, Dorothy, his wife was never fully able to deal with it. Her reaction to his illness had never been favorable, and when Sara had problems, Dorothy left. Of course, things in people's views had changed, but how much?

Bill arrived at his stop.

Meanwhile, Sara was slipping in her efforts to live well in the lodge.

"Sara, you missed your house duty, today," said Millie.

"I was planning on washing the dishes when we got home from work."

"Too late. We need the lunch dishes washed for the evening meal."

"You never told me."

"Sara. What are we going to do?"

At work.

"Sara, this hallway where you supposedly vacuumed doesn't look like it's even been done," said Lisa, Sara's coordinator and site boss.

"These vacuums have no suction power. We need new vacuums."

Walls were closing in around Sara. She hadn't been able to handle living with her father so she turned to the lodge. Now she was getting heat at the lodge. Sara thought about taking flight. She remembered a time when she had done that before.

"What's a sweet girl like you doing in Times Square looking like you just lost your best friend?" asked the raggedy old man who held a brown paper bag in one hand.

"I'm not just any girl you know."

Sara, a 17-year-old, was on the run. She had just escaped from a two-week stay at a hospital in Albany. Her father was in Los Angeles defending Randall Smith, a hugely successful blues artist, who was being sued in Civil Court.

"You are probably wondering why the Virgin Mary is wandering the streets."

The bum knew something was up with the young girl.

"Why, yes, I was wondering that."
"People think I'm going to screw up."
"They do? Why, yes, I believe they do."
"I'm not going to though. I've got it together now."
"Looks like you do."
"If I'm going to bring back Jesus to the earth…"

"Lady, you're WEIRD."

The man's words cut deeper than his actions which were to give her the finger and stick out his butt at her as he walked away. Sara was in mild shock. The man had been talking so gently, agreeing with her, then, as soon as she said her intentions she got that. *What's so bad about Jesus? Why the antagonism? The bum said he knew. Everyone knows. It's now or never. Jesus come to me.* With that, Sara seeking purity, some perfect refuge, a type of justifiable answer for her dilemma in the world, and unable to resist these urges, publicly disrobed.

She was quickly apprehended by police.

Now some five years later she knew she couldn't do that again. But where on earth could she find sanctuary? Where could she go? Who could she turn to?

At the Washington Lodge, on a night a few hours after getting home for work, Sara found herself knocking on the bedroom door of her lodge mate Jim.

"Jim?"
"Sara?"
"Jim, I know it's late…"
"It's O.K. What's up?" He opened the door. He was wearing pajamas.
"Oh, I'm sorry."
"It's O.K."
"I just…I mean. I'm a little nervous."
"Nervous? About what?"
"I don't know how to say it."
"What's on your mind, Sara?"
"I don't know if things are going to work out. I'm not in control of my life."

"Oh. Yeah. I know what you mean."

"What? I mean you know?"

"People been talking Sara."

"I guess I know."

"Yeah."

"Maybe I should sleep on it."

"If you can, I think it would be best."

4

Bain Bottles had been Sara's cohort for about two years. They met at the time Sara transitioned from the Washington Lodge back to her father's home in White Plains. Sara had been at the Washington Lodge for three years, from 17 to 20 years old. She had been satisfying a court deal that was made after it was determined that she was legally insane when she attempted to poison another patient while they were on a psych ward together. That, along with her public disrobing developed into an agreement. The agreement was that Sara would live for three years in a community mental health program. Her case was pre-Mental Health Court, but at a time when courts were beginning to consider alternative sentencing. She did her three years and moved back with her dad but continued employment through the Washington Lodge. She had met Bain on the streets of Manhattan. Tonight, they had gotten together for another reason.

> "Sara, hurry up."
> "Bain, I'm going as fast as I can."
> "If your father finds us stealing his car we're dead meat."
> "He always takes the train anyway."

Sara slid the key into the ignition and started the light blue Toyota Camry. She used the garage opener, backed down the driveway, and they were on the road.

> "Bain? Where are we going?"
> "West. We're heading West."
> "California?"
> "Sounds good."

What they didn't know was that the judge had heard the noise, looked out the window, and surmised what had happened.

"911."

"Yes, I want to report a stolen car."

Because Bain and Sara were both drunk and Sara couldn't drive straight, they soon caught the attention of the police who found out the car was registered to someone else, and they both were taken to Westchester County Jail after being on the road only 20 minutes.

"Hello, Lisa?"

"Is this Sara? Sara it's 2:00 A.M. What could you possibly think calling me at this hour?"

"Lisa, I'm in jail."

"Oh my God Sara. What did you do?"

"Me and my boyfriend just borrowed my father's car, and he reported it stolen. They're saying we…"

"Who's this boyfriend?"

"Bain Bottles."

"Oh Sara. Not him. Everyone at the lodge told you to stay away from him."

"Lisa, can you bail me out?"

"Sara, this is one mess you got yourself into that you're going to have to get yourself out of. Good night."

The jailer led Sara back to her cell.   Sara barely knew she was in jail. In her mind, at this point, little made sense. She could hold somewhat lucid conversations with a few choice people like Lisa who knew how to talk to her in a certain way. However, logic and reason escaped her, and she had no anchors in her thinking. The best she could do is react to what was in front of her, and for now all she knew was that she was locked up and couldn't flee which was her strongest desire. She couldn't say really what she was fleeing from or fleeing to – she just did anything to keep the adrenalin running and try to get thoughts flowing in her mind. In some ways, she was shut down. In other ways, she was over stimulated. She was out of the groove, and well beyond her comfort zone into something more like hysteria i.e. psychosis.

"Where's Bain? BAAIINN."

"Keep your mouth shut young lady," demanded the jailer.

"I want to see my lawyer."

"You'll see one soon enough."
"I can't think."
"That's obvious."
"Stop making fun of me."
"Lady, I don't even have to try."

The judge got a call the next day in his office.
"Mr. McCutcheon?"
"Yes."
"This is Officer Jackson of the White Plains Police. We've recovered your car. Sara was driving it."
"What about my daughter? What about Sara?"
"She's in jail right now."

"Oh my God. Is she O.K.?"

It was Sunday, the first Sunday after the first half-week Bill McCutcheon had worked as a judge. Sara had found out that Friday that she would be going back to the Washington Lodge. Bill and Sara sat formally at the dining room table. Bill had grilled a family steak and they had corn and toast and a salad. He had wine and she had ice tea.

"You were saying Sara…"
"I was saying a lot, but you never listen."
"That is not true. Sara, you accuse me of such things."
"No. It's you always the one trying to lay a guilt trip on me."
"I am?"
Bill knew he had to be gentle for a wrong word or a missed nuance might send Sara off and put distance between them that he didn't want to fathom. He was trying, oh God he was trying, to be supportive. Both from his experiences and what he had read and come into contact within his lifetime, he knew Sara was sick, and he refused to hold her fully accountable for that condition. It was a disease that Sara never asked for and certainly out of her control. Bill thought his best hope was to rebuild the Sara he once had known.

"Sara, what'd you learn in church today?"

Bill, Dorothy, and Sara had just come home on Sunday, and Bill was reaching out to his 12-year-old daughter.

"It was all about the Good Samaritan."
"So…"
"Everybody is my neighbor."

"Good Sara. That's a really good interpretation," said the 47-year-old defense attorney.

"Is that what you think, Dad?"

"Yes, I think that's a good..."

"No. I mean do you think everyone is your neighbor?"

"Well..."

"Would you help someone who was mugged?"

"I'd like to think..."

"Dad, I don't think even you can help everyone."

"Sara, you're wise to know that."

Bill, at the dinner table with 22-year-old Sara, felt like he was tied in knots. The last thing he wanted to do was make Sara feel guilty, yet she was adamantly determined in her mind that that is what he was doing.

"Bill, I look at you and I can just hear your words, 'Guilty, guilty, and guilty.'"

"Sara, I'm not..."

"The hell. You want me to share my life with the world."

"What?"

Bill was beginning to wish he'd not been so insistent on having their Sunday dinner. Would he ever be able to bring back his little girl? He remembered the time when he brought the big star Randall Smith in to talk with Sara. Smith had worked his magic, and Bill thought he had Sara. That lasted about one day. Then the illness took over again.

"Sara, I only want what is best for you."

"That is just a crock."

"What then?"

"You never believed I was the Virgin Mary. That I could be someone who could save the world."

"How could I believe that?"

"It was so good. So beautiful."

"But that's not who you are."

"Who cares?"

Sara was not sure she should have said that. Sara was flip about a lot of things, but she still had a healthy respect for how bad mental illness could be if she didn't take it seriously, that and her relationship with God which was quite non –traditional. She remembered being locked in solitary confinement and not having access to her medications. Her tenuous hold on reality had never been so tested. It was a horror story. She had stripped naked, eaten her poop, and banged her head against the wall. All this had been ignored by the jailers. She had been in jail for several months waiting for court orders to be transferred to a mental health facility. Then she had found the Washington Lodge. It was a godsend.

"Sara, don't you know I care."

"Then why wouldn't you let me be who I was?"

"Didn't I?"

"No. You said I was delusional."

"What are we talking about here?"

"The Virgin Mary. You said that was delusional."

"You being the Virgin Mary is delusional."

On the one side, you had the judge who was arguing to get his daughter back to some semblance of control. On the other side, you had the daughter who was staking out a big claim if you could see it that way rather than just a delusional girl. Bill was afraid Sara would never return to herself in her own lifetime. Sara was running away from herself as fast as she could. For both of them, at this juncture, the Washington Lodge was an answer. At the Washington Sara would not have to explain her thing with the Virgin Mary. The clients and the staff would not confront her on it if she could still work.

But after only a couple of weeks of rejoining the program, Sara was facing grand theft auto. There she sat, along with Bain, in front of their defense attorney.

"My father had said it was O.K. to borrow the car," lied, Sara.

Bain looked over and nodded his head.

The over-worked and under-slept defense attorney quickly said, "Your father…isn't your father a judge?"

Sara nodded.

"Your father," continued the lawyer, "reported it as stolen."

Just then the lawyer's cell phone rang.

"Just a sec'." "Hello, this is Darrell."

" Judge McCutcheon? "

"There's been a terrible mistake?"

"You had given your approval for your daughter to borrow the car whenever she wanted?"

"You're coming up to the jail to get the matter cleared up?"

"O.K. Judge. We'll be here."

"Sara, I don't know if you surmised…"

"It's what I've been telling you guys," lied, Sara.

In about an hour, the judge came into the room where the lawyer and the two would-be criminals sat. The judge got right down to business.

"It's all a mistake," said the judge. "I'm not pressing charges. There was no theft."

Sara and Bain were unable to look the judge in the eye. They both took a deep breath, and knew they'd been given some kind of huge break.

"Judge McCutcheon, the obvious question is why did you report the car as stolen?"

"I didn't know it was Sara."

The judge was cool as ice and never really looked at his daughter or Bain, but instead addressed the lawyer.

"Can I bail them out until we get the thing cleared up?"

"Sure, Judge. Sure."

On the way home Sara was in the judge's second car, and Bain drove the vehicle in question. Sara and her father never spoke.

Dorothy, Bill's separated wife, and Sara's mother, had taken an apartment in Manhattan when she had left the family five years ago. She had struggled on her own, but Bill sent her some money. The rest she earned at Temps.

"My ex is a big-time judge," said Dorothy one afternoon at break to another Temps worker.

"Then what are you doing working?" the woman asked.

"Oh, he gives me some money, if that's what you mean," replied Dorothy.

"Apparently not enough."

"Well..."

"My ex didn't have much money, but I did get the house up in Queens. I made sure of that."

"Well..."

"Come 'mon girl. Get with the program."

Up in Harlem, a cop in a small grocery store was catching Willie thieving a packet of donuts. He saw Willie stick the bakery goods under his coat and waited for Willie to exit. As soon as Willie went out the door, the cop followed.

"Hey, Willie," said the black police officer to the black offender. "What have you got under your coat?"

"Oh, damn. I didn't mean no harm."

What the cop knew, and what everybody that was familiar with the neighborhood knew, was that Willie had a rap sheet as long as a yard stick. He was one of the least fortunate classes of people, the chronically mentally ill. Sometimes he was on medication, but most often not. He drank whenever he could and ate good food less often than that. Most times he would just end up in jail.

However, this time was different. When the wheels turned he was offered a chance at the Mental Health Court. It was the longest of a long shot, like a four or five pointer in basketball.

"Willie," said the prosecutor to the 45-year-old man, "Do you want the chance of your lifetime?"

They were sitting together in a room at Rikers along with Gonzalez a frequent defense attorney at the Mental Health Court.

"Yeah, golldarnit. I'll do anything to change."

"How long is it Willie since you first got diagnosed?"

"Dia-what?"

"Since you've worked or had a home?"

"Ten or fifteen."

"That's a long time."

"Hey. I've got my pride. What'cha mean?"

"No one is questioning that Willie. But don't you get tired of this?"

"Yeah. I get tired."

Willie looked up at the attorney with unfocused and half-determined eyes.

"We're going to give you a chance, Willie."

"At what, Judge?"

The two attorneys told Willie about the Manhattan Mental Health Court. They explained that he had to stop drinking, get on medication, and get a job.

"Now where am I gonna find a job?" asked Willie.

"You can push a broom can't you?"

In a couple short weeks, Willie stood before Judge McCutcheon in court. He was accompanied by Gonzalez, a prosecutor, and a case worker.

"So, Willie, tell me. Are you going to be able to do this?"

"Judge, it's my last chance. I know that."

"That doesn't answer my question, Willie."

"What? Do you want some kind of comentment?"

"Yes. Something like commitment."

"Well, I don't know…"

"Maybe we've asked the wrong man."

"No."

Willie straightened himself up and the eyes that were unfocused and glazed suddenly saw some light.

"I'll do it golldarnit. I'll do it."

What could the State lose? Willie with his frequent visits to jails and hospital emergency rooms was already costing the taxpayers a lot of money. If he was able to turn his life around he could conceivably get to a point of giving back. What a victory that'd be.

5

"Mom, this is Sara."

"Where are you calling from?"

"I borrowed the coach's cell phone. I'm calling from White Plains soccer field."

"What are you doing on the soccer field? You know we're having Sunday dinner."

"Yeah but I wanted to be with the team."

"Sara, you're not even a player. You're only the manager."

"Daddy told me it is a very important job."

"But Sara…"

"Can't we move dinner up to this evening?"

Bill was riding the train home some several weeks into the advent of the Mental Health Court. He was reading of a personal account of a woman who had developed schizophrenia, then lost her job, became homeless, then recovered to become a program director in a mental health agency.

I wondered what was happening to me. Here I was in my 20's in my first job after school and having trouble. I was a loan officer for veterans. I had to clear paperwork so the ex-soldiers could get home and school loans. This required that I talk to the vets to get information. I was forgetting facts and figures that I at one time had mastered.

Bill thought that Sara was not doing even challenging enough work to be forgetful at it.

My boss began to notice. When he asked me about it, I had no answer. I decided to see a doctor who referred me to a psychiatrist who diagnosed me with schizophrenia. In a short while I went into the hospital. I lost my insurance because my boss let me go. They discharged me and I went back to my apartment, but I had no income. I had applied for Social Security Disability and Medicare at the hospital. Eventually I was accepted and got some money, but it wasn't enough to hold my apartment. I had to give it up, and I became homeless.

Bill knew that Sara would be homeless if it wasn't for him and the Washington Lodge.

My life became hell. I ate anything I could get my hands on including food at soup kitchens and out of garbage cans. I also slept at occasional shelters, on park benches, and in cardboard boxes.

Sara thinks she's got it rough?

I could see no end in sight. My days were drudgery. Most nights were sleepless. Then came my miracle. One day, some six months after I had been homeless, I saw a sign posted at a shelter: Help Wanted – person to clean my home. Something inside of me jumped. I applied for the job, and I got it. Then I began to move up.

I think Washington Lodge is Sara's miracle, if she can only stick with it.

"Sara, can you help me with dinner?"

"I know. Dad has to watch the game."

"Sara, I wish for you that someday you'll have a husband who isn't a sports junkie."

Bain was not really husband material, but he was a junkie.

"Sara, be careful."

Sara had bumped the mirror that held four lines of cocaine. Bain had just arranged them with a razor blade. The mirror sat on a chair which was between Sara and Bain who sat on Sara's bed in the Tudor mansion. Sara had been suspended for a day from work for swearing at Lisa when Lisa had criticized her work. It was a Wednesday afternoon. The judge was in court.

"I am sooo glad they don't do drug testing at Washington Lodge," Sara said with a smile.

"Would you even be a part of it if they did?" asked Bain who rolled up a dollar bill into a straw and snorted two lines.

"What else could I do Bain? The judge won't be around forever."

"I mean if you couldn't do drugs, what would you…?"

Sara took the straw and snorted the other two lines.

"My old man thinks I'm on the straight and narrow."

They both laughed.
"I've got to admit, I was quite surprised when he got us off the hook for the car last week," said Bain.
"My dad is a fool. I've got him wrapped around my little finger."

They laughed again. Then they fell back on the bed and had sex.
A man with a long history of hospitalizations for mental illness sat in his room in Brooklyn drinking out of a quart bottle of gin. There was a twin mattress on the floor with some moth-eaten blankets thrown over it. In a corner was a one-cup coffee maker with a coffee stained pot. The window looked out onto a brick wall. The shade was broken. The gray paint on the walls was peeling. In a word – dump.

Brent Jones looked over to the one wall where an assault rifle lied against it. He walked over to the gun. Off the floor he picked up a clip, which held 30 rounds. He took a long green duffle bag and slid in the rifle and clip. He threw on his coat, and put the duffle bag over his shoulder. He bent down and picked up pen and paper. He wrote four words, "HOLY WAR HAS BEGUN".

As he was leaving through the hallway, the landlady, Miss Everett, came out of her door. The two exchanged glances, but Miss Everett quickly retired back to her room. She hadn't liked the looks of things so she quickly called the police. She explained her concern. She described Jones and told the dispatcher that he had headed north probably to get on the subway.

Two police cars soon converged on the neighborhood. One of them spotted Jones who surrendered without resistance.

Judge McCutcheon got word of the incident the next day. Scott Jensen, the prosecutor, related to the judge the police report.

"There's one who is never going to make it to Mental Health Court."

"I can see why you say that Scott, but what more do we know about him?"

"What do you need to know? A man loads up headed to shoot up people…what more do you need to know?"

"Like perhaps, did he seek help and get refused?"

"I can't believe you."

"And I can't believe you either. Are we still civilized? Or are we barbarians?"

"A man intends grievous harm…"

"Because he is a man out of control. I mean what more do we know about him?"

"Your faith in mankind is a lot higher mountain than I'm willing to climb."

"And that's why I'm a judge. It's philosophical, Scott. I believe the good outweighs the bad unless it's proven otherwise."

"I believe you are the most naïve man I've met."

"Mr. Jensen, I am a human being and all that that means."

"Good day Judge."

"And I'll be looking for some kind of report from you on this Mr. Jones."

"Sara, I am so glad you had that talk with Randall."

Sara and Bill were having their Sunday dinner when Sara was a 17-year-old. Sara had had a heart-to-heart with Randall Smith. Smith was a superstar blues musician whose fame spanned decades with a loyal following that included Bill McCutcheon. Bill had had a dream come true when he became Smith's defense attorney in a civil suit. Then, when Bill started having trouble with Sara, he arranged a meeting with Smith and Sara thinking the sheer star power of Smith could restore Bill's relationship with Sara.

"It was no big thing Dad. Well, I guess it was Randall Smith all right."

"Randall told me you were touched."

"Touched? I don't know. Yeah. Well kind of."

"Randall told me he was quite proud to know you."

"Really? He said that?"

"Yes, Sara. He really said that."

The two had almost stopped eating. Bill was trying so hard to keep himself in Sara's life without being forceful, overbearing, or parenty. Sara seemed indifferent about it. It was not lost on Bill that his daughter said she thought she was the Virgin Mary. Yet, Bill could see a side of Sara that really didn't believe the delusion. It was as if the delusion was something that had been thrust upon Sara that she could not deal with alone. In Bill's heart, he didn't believe she wanted the delusion but felt resigned, if not forced, into it. Bill's vision of her was that she was his little girl.

Sara was quite unstable. It was about a year ago her mind began to become unhinged. She lost her focus and her concentration. Then she began to hear voices that were intrusive and unsettling. If a radio was on, she thought the people were talking about her. When she went places, she thought everyone could read her thoughts as if her mind was an open book. Most of the voices were negative. If she overheard a conversation and someone said something like, "she's such a dork", well Sara thought it was about her. About the only positive voice was that of God who Sara interpreted as telling her she was the Virgin Mary. She clung to that and ignored the others.

"Yeah, Mr. Smith, told me to be myself. What do you think of that?"

"I think that's good advice."

"Then why do you insist on telling me I'm not Mary."

"Wait a minute. When I say yourself, I mean Sara McCutcheon."

"She's gone. That's who I used to be. That's old stuff."

"Sara nobody believes you're the Virgin Mary."

"The people on the radio do."

"Who?"

"The musicians. They send me messages in their lyrics."

"Personal messages?"

"Yes."

"You think they know who you are?"

"Yes." Sara said that but had her doubts.

"I don't think they know you from Eve."

At this point Sara began to get a feeling of being crushed. The world she had created, her private deepest self, was being trounced by her father. Bill was sure he was right to break down any delusions. He had forgotten his youth when he believed Randall Smith was sending him messages.

"Mr. McCutcheon, you have got to snap out of these delusionary thoughts."

Bill, an 18- year-old, was in front of the group in a psych ward in Boston. He was being addressed by another patient. He was in the hot seat.

"I think Randall Smith is sending me messages." Bill stood firm.

"Then why isn't he here? Why hasn't he come to the hospital to see you?"

"He's a busy man."

"He doesn't care about you?"

"He cares about everyone."

"You really think so?"

"That's what I said."

"You think he cares more about you than we do?"

"If you cared about me you wouldn't be putting so much pressure on me."

"Who's putting pressure on you? I'm just asking questions. And how about Smith? Isn't he putting pressure on you?"

"I don't know, I…"

"You've got to decide. It's us or him."

Those were the hardest moments a young Bill McCutcheon lived through. It was torture to see it happening to Sara.

6

"Molly, I told a lie to the police to get Sara off the hook."

Molly and the judge were in his chambers a couple days after the car theft.

"Oh Bill. My God. I mean you're a judge. What did she do?"

The judge explained the circumstances.

"Bill you astound me. What you tell me you do for her. I always thought of you as a saint but this is beyond sainthood. Do you realize you're putting your career on line? I mean I can see the headline, "Judge lies to protect daughter".

"Isn't that what her mind is doing to her now? Her mind is telling her lies."

"So, you're going to compound the lies?"

"I'll do anything to help…anything."

"O.K. Bill. All right. Do what you have to do. I'll stand by you. I have for 20 years. I won't stop now."

"Harder, Bain. Harder. Screw me good."

"Sara, you're so tight."

Sara and Bain were having one of their matinees while the judge worked away in court. When they were done, they collapsed in laughter.

"If only Billie Willie could see me now," said Sara.
"The old guy'd flip his wig." Bain smirked.
They laughed some more.
"I have to admit it was nice of the old guy to cover for us last week about the car and everything," said Bain.
"My dad is a fool. He'd do anything for me…anything."
"What time do you have to be back at the Washington Lodge?" asked Bain.
"What time is it? Oh God, I have a half hour. Let's get dressed Bain. Hurry. You have to take me."
"You think I'm like your father? I'll do anything…anything? Just kidding."

Lisa was at the front door of the lodge looking at her watch when Sara and Bain pulled up.
"You're 15 minutes late Sara. You've held up the work van again. This time it will be the decision of the lodge as to whether you're still in the program."
Sara pleaded, "I have no alternative. Where else can I go?"
"We're going to make you think long and hard about that Sara. Now get in the van."
Sara got into the van and was met with icy stares from the rest of the Lodge group.
"Hi guys. Thanks for waiting."
Nobody said another word the rest of the trip to work.

When they got to the county building Sara went to her locker and put on her work shirt. As she was leaving the locker room Millie stood in the aisle blocking her way.

"You're through Sara. Your goose is cooked."

Sara brushed past her. She went and got her vacuum and started her route. In her mind, she was the victim. Wasn't the burden on her? Not only had God told her she was the Virgin Mary, now He had set everyone against her. Who could she confide in? Not Bain. It wasn't the kind of relationship they had. Yet she felt a need. God was too immense, too distant to feel any sense of security. There was Jim, the sandy haired boy, but he had his own problems.

"Hi there."

One of the county employees was working late in an office where Sara was assigned to vacuum.

"Oh hi. My name is Sara. Is it O.K. to vacuum?"

"My name is Betty. Nice to meet you. Are you doing all right?"

Sara wondered if her instability was so apparent.

"Yes, I'm fine."

"So, you're one of the Washington Lodge crew. We sure love you guys doing our cleaning."

"I may not be here too much longer," said Sara.

"Now why is that?"

Sara, in her disabled mind, thought Betty already knew, and was just asking her the question to put the pressure on her. Nonetheless, she answered the question.

"I can't seem to get along with my co-workers."

"You seem perfectly fine to me."

Sara was a little surprised. Was Betty just being sarcastic, or was it possible that she really didn't know and was just being nice. Sara decided to take it that way.

"Why thank you. I'll vacuum now."

With that Sara switched on the vacuum and Betty shut off the overhead light above her desk and left. Sara thought to herself, either she is egging me on or she really doesn't know I'm the Virgin Mary. This caused Sara to go back in time to when she first got the idea that she was the Virgin Mary.

"Sara, you are the worst soccer player I've ever seen." Veronica was a loud-mouthed girl who said just about anything. They were on the White Plains athletic field on a crisp fall day. Sara sought to crawl into a shell, but out of the corner of her eye, she saw an elderly woman walking on the sidewalk nearby who smiled at her. At that moment, Sara had an epiphany. Like a shroud over her head and a glow, Sara had a warmth come into her heart and mind which she interpreted as an angel communicating to her that she was the Virgin Mary. It made sense because Sara was a virgin, and the name Sara was a little like the name Mary. Eureka!

From that moment on, Sara had clung to her revelation like a stamp to a letter. The moniker had traveled with her despite her losing her virginity, which she did with Bain, and despite the fact she hadn't set foot in a church for several years. Sara, to think of herself as the Virgin Mary, gave her the last bastion of any goodness in her soul. It was as far as she would retreat towards total darkness. Plus, it had been the initiative of the angel, and Sara could do little to stop it.

The next day at work, Betty, the county worker, was there late again.

"Hi Sara," Betty beamed as Sara opened the door of the room and entered, a vacuum in hand.

"Hi Betty. I just gotta vacuum if that's O.K."

"Fine." Betty smiled an inviting smile. "Say you look a little more cheerful today."

"Well it is Friday."

Sara unwound the cord and started to walk towards the outlet.

"Hold it a sec," said Betty. "Before you get started tell me what you're going to do this weekend."

Sara froze. She knew she would probably be getting together with Bain and have sex and drink and do drugs. Sara knew she could never tell Betty this.

"I'll probably hang out at the Lodge."

"What's the Lodge again?"

"It's the group home where the people who I work with here, live."

"Oh, I didn't know you folks lived together."

"Work and live together. It's kind of cool."

Sara surprised herself. Had she actually said the Lodge was cool? She went on.

"It's the Fairweather Lodge Model. It's based on the peer support people with mental illness give one another. It's like a commune."

"That does sound cool," said Betty surprisingly sounding like she understood and accepted what a commune was. "So, I suppose you get to know each other quite well."

Nevertheless, Sara was beginning to get uncomfortable feeling she was deceiving Betty.

"Betty, if you don't mind I better start my vacuuming or I'll get behind."

"Sure Sara. We'll talk on Monday and you can tell me how the weekend went."

"Judge McCutcheon there is just no way Brent Jones is a candidate for mental health court."

McCutcheon and the prosecutor Jensen were in the judge's chambers about a week after Jones had been apprehended. The judge had read the police report and had talked with a case worker who was familiar with Jones.

"Scott, the weapon was registered. He's been held on a charge of making a terroristic threat to his landlord, but even his landlord says he didn't say anything to her. He broke no laws. Maybe he was going target-shooting."

"You're really something. You know that. What does it take before you give up on someone? Is everyone capable of rehabilitation?"

"I think so."

Jensen buried his face in his hands, then looked at the judge with pleading eyes, "Please don't ask me to do this one. For the love of God. Please don't."

"We have a man with mental illness who was carrying a gun..."

"Didn't you see the report? 'HOLY WAR HAS BEGUN'. They found his note in his room. Doesn't sound like target-shooting to me."

"If everyone who ever made a statement in rage, 'I'll murder you' was put in jail, there'd be no one outside of jail."

"Judge, I'll talk to Gonzales. See if she thinks she could defend him. We have to do a screening and assessment..."

"I'm not saying, 'Go ahead'. I'm just saying let's take a look. Feel the guy out."

"I do believe you are the nicest and most naïve guy I know. Good day, Judge."

7

It hit the front page of the New York Times – above the fold.
DOES JUDGE LIE TO GET HIS DAUGHTER OFF?
McCutcheon didn't know until he picked up the morning paper on the way to work. The reporter had tried to reach the judge both at work and at home, but Bill had told Molly to hold all calls because of his heavy involvement in the Brent Jones case and at home, he hadn't checked messages for days because he had been trying to take care of Sara.

Bain had spilled the beans when he had been arrested for possession of a small amount of marijuana. The drug user and dealer had requested to speak to Scott Jensen's office, and he told him about Judge McCutcheon's little lie a couple of weeks earlier. Of course Jensen had balked at giving Bain an easier bargain, but he gleefully received the information and went to the paper. The editor of the Times was ambivalent about the Mental Health Court. While he saw some good, he thought that it was an evasion of justice and wrist-slapping. He was willing to print the article not feeling a need to protect McCutcheon even though nothing had been proven.

When the judge got to the office, Molly met him at the elevator.

"Oh Bill. I'm so sorry."
"Anybody called yet?"
"Jensen's called three times."
"It's only 7:30. He's called three times?"

With that Bill retired to his chambers. He had barely sat down when Molly buzzed him to tell him Jensen was on the line.

"Oh, hi Scott."
"Bill, you don't have to tell me if you don't want to, but did you read this morning's paper?"
"As a matter of fact, I did," Bill said coldly.
"You sound upset."
Bill couldn't fathom the statement.
After five seconds he asked, "Was it you?"
"Yes."
"Scott, why?"
"It's the truth. Citizens have a right to know."
"How did you know?"
"That Bain fellow. Your daughter's boyfriend. He was picked up for possession of marijuana."
"Scott, did you give him a deal for that?"
"No. I wouldn't do that to you, Bill."
Again, Bill couldn't fathom the comment.
Jensen asked, "Well the big question is, 'Was Bain telling the truth?'"
"I'm not going to answer that right now, Scott."
"Oh…yeah…right. When you decide to talk let me know."
Bill hung up and buzzed Molly and asked her to come into his chambers.
"Bill. What did Jensen have to say?"
Bill knew he could count on Molly.
"He's decided to take advantage of the situation let's say."
"Bill, what are you going to do?"

"Tell the truth."

"Are you sure? I mean what are the facts?"

"I knew Sara and Bain stole my car. I reported it stolen. Then I changed my mind. I told the police that they had my permission."

"I'm not even going to get into why you're protecting Sara, but you've got to protect yourself. Some things you just have to keep to yourself."

"Molly it's my personal integrity. The papers, the public, I can't lie to them."

"Bill, you told the police a lie."

"I know. It was a mistake."

"Well if you tell everyone, won't Sara go to jail?"

"I'd hope the authorities won't charge her. I won't press charges."

"Bill. I admire your courage…but question your wisdom."

The next day the Times article read,
"JUDGE ADMITS FIBBING TO POLICE".
Judge Bill McCutcheon has admitted he was aware that his daughter and boyfriend stole his car a week ago which goes contrary to the story he originally told the police. The judge only hoped it wouldn't set off Sara even more.

It was Monday morning at the county building and Sara had just started to head to work when Millie stopped her in the hallway.

"I would have thought a judge would tell the truth."

"What are you talking about Millie?"

"What everyone else in New York is talking about. Your daddy is a liar."

"What?!"

"It's in the paper. Your father lied to get you off from a charge of auto theft."

With that Millie walked away.

When Sara went to Betty's office to vacuum, her head was reeling.

Betty was there and greeted her promptly.

"Hi Sara. How was the weekend? Did you spend it with your Lodgemates?"

"Matter of fact I did," lied Sara because the last thing she wanted to do was to have Betty know about things.

"Oh yeah. What'd you do?"

"We went out to a movie and had dinner."

"Oh yeah. What'd you see?"

Sara paused then said, "That new Harry Potter movie," thinking that it sounded quite wholesome.

"Oh, there's sorcery in those movies."

"Yeah," said Sara a little off-balance.

"It's of the Devil," said Betty with conviction.

"Yeah, I know what you mean," said Sara shifting.

"You don't like the Devil's work do you Sara?"

"Oh no. Not me."

Sara's mind went back immediately to her belief she was the Virgin Mary. She tried to feign shock.

"Well that's good. Satan is already working way too hard in this world."

With that Betty shut off her desk light and said goodbye. Sara stood there a couple of minutes almost dumbfounded as to what as just transpired. Only she could know the tension in her being between who she was and who Betty thought she was.

"Me the Virgin Mary? How can I be?" she mumbled to herself.

Yet, there was still part of her that remembered some five years earlier the comfort this belief had once given her. She had clung to the belief through drug addiction, psychosis, and Bain. She knew she wasn't orthodox, but she still believed that she held a special place in God's world.

"Hello Bill?"

McCutcheon immediately recognized his ex-wife's voice.

"Hi Dorothy."

"Bill, I want to come out to the house to see you."

"What's the occasion?" Bill asked, curious as to why she was contacting him.

"Can't tell you now. Let's just set a date."

"How about this coming Sunday…for dinner?"

"That'd be great. And make sure Sara is there."

"Hello Judge McCutcheon. This is Joshua Seiling from the governor's office."

"Oh yes, Joshua. What can I do for you?"

Bill was cordial.

"It's about this article in the Times that I have in front of me. What gives?"

"I'm glad you called me. The whole thing is true," said Bill matter-of-factly.

"What? And you're admitting it?"

Seiling was going for the throat.

"Yep. I refuse to cover up a mistake I made. The article has all the facts straight."

Bill was as honest as a $5 dollar bill.

"Well, well. I'll just tell you the governor is interested in this one. I don't know what will happen. You could be fined, or suspended, even removed."

"Whatever goes down, at least I'll be clean."

Bill had found strength in his resolution to protect Sara.

"Bill, I admire your courage. I'll be getting back to you."

In the subway car on the way home, Bill did not pull out any books, magazines, or newspapers. He grabbed a seat, leaned back, and closed his eyes. It occurred to him that someone might recognize him from the picture in the newspaper. What was the public sentiment going to be? Could a father's love for his daughter trump his dishonesty? In his heart, he hadn't really felt he was dishonest. There were just two different answers to two separate times. His first reaction had been to implicate Sara and Bain. After he thought about it he had chose not to incriminate them. Was he guilty in this scenario or a hero? Would the public be sympathetic?

That Sunday Sara showed up at the house before Dorothy who was only a couple of minutes behind. When she came through the door Bill quickly realized that she was all business.

"Bill. Sara. Why don't we have a seat at the dining room table."

Normally, Bill would have been hesitant to take orders from Dorothy in his own home, but he was truly curious as to the business at hand, so he acquiesced.

"Bill," Dorothy wasted no time, "I want the house."

After the shock, Bill stared at her and said, "Dorothy, you can't be serious."

"I'm as serious as a brick."

"But...Dorothy..."

"Bill when we were separated we made an agreement or have you forgotten?"

"Forgotten?" said Bill. "I've sent you money."

"It's not enough Bill. The agreement which I have a copy of says you would take care to ensure the lifestyle that Sara and I were used to."

"Sara's O.K."

Sara, for once in her life was speechless, but was intently watching the drama unwind.

"Bill she's bouncing around in some God-awful hippie commune and has not been able to accomplish anything in her life. If I had the house with Sara, I would make sure she made something out of her life."

"The Washington Lodge? A hippie commune?"

Bill had decidedly been caught off-guard. He hated to trust his instincts here because his instincts told him to ask Sara, and he knew the volatility of their relationship. However, he saw the look in Sara's eyes that he hadn't seen in many years. It was a look of kindness, sympathy, and gentleness.

Bill asked, "Sara what do you think about all of this?"

Sara's answer would truly surprise everyone present, including herself.

"I won't go along with Dad losing the house. At least he's trying to be a parent."

Then Sara took a measured look at Dorothy.

"Mom you abandoned me. You abandoned both of us. There is just no way I'll go along with your plan."

Dorothy knew she was beat. She grabbed the copy of the agreement to ownership of the house that she had drafted and tore it in pieces.

"Well. I won't take any more of your time."

She stood up, walked over to the door, and exited.

Sara and Bill sat at the table in utter amazement at what had just happened.

Sara finally spoke.

"Bill, don't get any ideas. I'm not going soft. I just don't like Mom."

Bill tried to understand what it would be like for someone to be forced to take sides in an argument between her parents. That was worse than any trial case he had ever been in.

All he could say was, "Sara, thanks."

Now he could turn his attention to his job and the governor - if he still had a job.

8

The judge was in his chambers when Joshua Seiling from the governor's office called.

"Bill, how are you today?"

"I'm fine."

"Bill, the governor is not pleased."

"I did what I thought was right."

"But it's out in the public now. We feel we have to act."

"What's going to happen?"

"We're going to relieve you of your duties."

"What?"

"For two weeks."

"Then what?"

"You'll go back on your job on a probationary basis for one year."

Bill had thought it was going to be worse. They were being gentle. They weren't throwing the book at him.

"What's going to happen with the Mental Health Court?"

"It'll be in recess."

Bill thought about his case load especially Brent Jones. It would have to wait. Bill used his two weeks off to spend time with Sara. It was Sunday, and Sara came through the front door of the home.

"Hi Bill," said Sara.

The judge outwardly ignored the greeting, and he focused his attention on the table which had already been set. He just had to get the food from the kitchen. Then they were both seated.

"Bill, just cause I saved you your house doesn't mean…"

Bill quickly changed gears.

"What are you going to do when you don't have me to kick around, Sara?"

"What?' asked a suddenly shocked Sara.

"What's going to happen when you can't blame me?"

"Dad, what are you saying?"

"I think it's quite clear. In your mind, it is me. Everything comes down to me. You treat me like I'm a door mat you can wipe your feet off with."

"Dad this doesn't sound like you," said Sara struggling for diplomacy.

"Doesn't sound like me? How much longer do you think I'll tolerate your behavior?"

"Well Dad I'm sorry if…"

"No, I don't think you really are, Sara, because you see only yourself."

"But, Dad, I've got a mental illness."

"I did too when I was your age…"

"What? Dad? You?"

"It's something your mother and I chose not to tell you."

"But you're a judge…you're successful."

"You seem to think mental illness is synonymous with failure."

"Dad, you're being hard on me."

"And you're not being hard on me?"

"Dad, I'm fragile."

"Yes, I believe you are. However, that does not allow you to unload on me."

"Dad, I'm sorry. I'll do better."

They ate the rest of their dinner in silence.

When they finished, Sara got up and said, "I'll be going now."

"How are you getting back to the Lodge?"

"Bain."

"Is that how you got here?"

"Yes."

"I want you to see him less often."

"But Dad…"

"He's not good for you."

"Can't I choose my own friends?"

"Make the choices you will. Just don't rely on me to support them."

Sara called Bain on her cell phone, and he was there in 15 minutes.

On her way out, Sara said, "If you think I'm crazy and that's it, I don't want to talk to you again," and she was gone.

Bill sat at the table for a half hour before he moved.

When he finally got up, he went to his bedroom, grabbed his sweats, and headed to the YMCA. He hadn't worked out for over five years, but today was different. He wasn't sure if he was burning off stress or strengthening himself for the task of supporting Sara's recovery. The ball was in Sara's court, and no one knew if she would show up to play.

A couple of weeks later, the judge was back in his chambers. Molly buzzed him. Jensen, the prosecutor, was on the line.

"Welcome back Bill."

McCutcheon wasn't really sure how to handle it; he decided to be friendly.

"Yeah, Scott. It's great to be back."

"Time away O.K.?"

"Yeah, spent time with my daughter."

"Well, anyway. Back to Brent Jones. Are you really serious about giving this guy a chance?"

"Doesn't everyone deserve a chance?"

"He's had his chances in life like everyone else. He's decided to make some pretty bad choices."

"Do you really think people with mental illness are capable of making a choice?"

"If not they shouldn't be out in public where they can be a danger."

"You're going back to the 1950's. Are you really saying that all people with mental illness should be in institutions? I thought you were in favor of Mental Health Court."

"It's people like Jones that make me wonder."

"Look Scott, if people with the illness can get medication and into recovery, well then they're like everyone else. Are we in America or not?"

"Don't tell me about rights. Jones had the right to seek treatment but he didn't."

"How do you know? Did you investigate? A lot of times people like Jones are turned away from help. Do you know for certain he didn't try to get help?"

"Well…no. I don't know."

"Then how can you consider him unfit for Mental Health Court?"

"It doesn't feel right to me."

"Doesn't feel right? Is that what you're saying?"

"Bill, let me sleep on it. I'll get back to you tomorrow."

Brent Jones was at Rikers Island jail an hour after being arrested.

"We're putting you in your own cell so nobody hurts you," said the guard.

"How long do I have to stay here?" asked Jones.

"As strange as you are it'll probably be a long time."

"Who you calling strange?" said Jones, as he contorted his face and gave the guard the finger.

"We know how to handle trouble-makers. We won't let a doctor see you."

"What would I need a doctor for?"

"The fact that you don't know proves what an idiot you are."

"And the trouble with cops is that they're fascists."

The guard turned and left.

It started with a few swear words, then a longer rant, and then a rage. After that Jones began banging his head against the wall.

Soon he was bleeding and in a daze. He fell to the floor exhausted.

Nobody was there to help him up.

"Bain, Bill's coming down on me," said Sara as they drove towards Long Island and the Washington Lodge after Sara's last Sunday dinner.

"What are we going to do?"

"Maybe I shouldn't see you for a while," said Sara with a trembling voice.

"You going to let your ol' man win?"

"I don't know Bain, but why did you have to rat him out about the car theft thing?"

"What?"

"Bain, you can't deny it. Everyone knows it was you who told the lawyer about my dad getting us off."

"I did it for us. I mean I thought you and your father…"

"He's still my dad."

"And who am I?"

"I want you to be my friend, Bain. You have to let go."

"OK,ok." Bain pulled over right on the highway and said, "Then get out."

"But Bain. I'm ten miles from home."

"You're the one who wants out, so get out." He had a fierce look that scared even Sara.

She got out.

"Lisa, this is Sara."

"What? I'm only a few miles away."

"Call somebody else?"

"OK."

"Jim, this is Sara. Do you still have van privileges for the Lodge?"

"This IS an emergency."

"Okay. I'll meet you in New Rochelle at the Comfort Inn. Know it?"

"Okay a half hour. Thanks, Jim. You're a lifesaver."

"What? Of course I mean it."

That Monday, Sara headed to the office, a little excited to see Betty.

"Hey Betty," greeted Sara as she came into the room with her vacuum.

"Well Sara! How was the weekend?"

"Great! Had Sunday dinner with my father."

"Did you stay out of trouble?"

"What?...why sure...why do you ask?"

"Oh, I didn't mean anything by it. There's so much trouble going on around, it's hard to avoid it."

"Oh I do my best."

"That's my girl."

Sara cringed, but not enough that Betty noticed.

"Well I guess I'll plug in," said Sara.

"Plug in?" asked Betty.

"The vacuum. Plug in the vacuum."

"Oh, of course. Have a great night, Sara."

Betty grabbed her purse and coat and left.

Sara's mind was in a tizzy. She was spilt in two, maybe three. Betty thought she was a wholesome young lady. Bain thought she was a tramp. The judge thought she was some of each. However, her dad wanted her to be a young lady, and Betty already thought she was. Bain was the only one who wanted her in the role of a floozy.

But what do I want? Becoming a woman has its good points, but Bain is more fun. I want fun. Wait a minute. Going to jail isn't fun. Getting thrown out of a car in the middle of nowhere isn't fun. Sex with Bain is fun. Drugs and alcohol with Bain is fun. So, what is it? Sex and drugs or respectable life? I want respect. Can I leave sex and drugs behind? How bad do I want respect? I need Dad's respect. I want to have some standards. I need standards. I've been selfish. What have I done to Dad?

This could have gone on a great deal longer, but Sara had finished vacuuming. She had to get ready to go home.

Once in the van, Sara could not keep silent.
"Jim, turn off the radio. I got something to say."
Everyone got deadly silent. They were expecting another rant from Sara.
"You guys, I want to say this. I need to say this. I've been bad to you. I haven't carried my weight, and I've been a bitch. What I want to say is I'm going to improve. Tonight, it starts to get better. There. Now turn back on the radio."

The Lodgemates exchanged glances, but no one was quite sure what to believe. Sara had made her confessions before, and gone back to her old ways. She hadn't been trustworthy. She'd let them down time and again. It was really a miracle she was still in the program. Sara knew all this and had made the decision as though her life was at the crossroads. If she didn't choose a path tonight, she never would. She knew it would take a while to convince the others and especially Lisa. She knew she didn't deserve the chance to redeem herself. She was just like the defendants in her dad's Mental Health Court. Here she was seeking mercy, mercy she had not usually given anyone else. Would she get it?

"Bill, it's a nurse from Rikers," said Molly over the intercom. "I usually screen these calls but she sounds desperate."

"OK. Put her through."

The woman came on the line. "Judge McCutcheon, I'm a nurse at Rikers, and there's a patient I just have to tell you about. His name is Brent Jones."

"Oh? I know the name."

"We have to get him to your Mental Health Court."

"Is that why you're calling?"

"He's being treated like garbage."

"Oh?"

"And I know he's sick and needs help. He didn't do anything."

"Yes. I've been working on his case myself."

"Then you know. We've got to get him his medication."

"He doesn't have meds?"

"Oh no. He's being treated like dirt."

"Let me see what I can do."

"Oh, thank you, Judge McCutcheon. Thank you so much."

The judge was soon on the line to the warden at Rikers.

"Warden, this is Judge McCutcheon from the Manhattan Mental Health Court."

"Oh, no it's not a special occasion. It's about one of your inmates, Brent Jones."

"The goofy one? Is that what you said? Warden, I expect more decorum from someone in your position."

"What do I want? First of all, this person needs to be on medication."

"You have dozens like him? O.K. let's take them one at a time. I'm calling right now specifically for Brent Jones.

"That's too bad about all the others, but this call, this time, I want Brent Jones to be seen by a doctor sooner than later. Then we'll deal with the others."

When they got back to the Lodge, Sara immediately went to the kitchen, and she began doing dishes.

Millie could not contain herself.

"Well, well, Sara. You're starting out strong, but I don't think it will last. How long are you going to be good? One week? One day?"

"We'll see, Millie. Now if you excuse me, I'm going to sweep the floor."

"Lord have mercy."

The next morning Sara got up early and did 50 sit-ups. She was exhausted. *Have to get that up to 100,* she thought. She went over to the phone.

"Dad, it's me."

"No, I'm fine."

"Yes, I'm sure."

"I just wanted to tell you that I did 50 sit-ups without a rest."

"Yes, that is why I called."

"No big deal? Dad, I thought you'd be proud."

"Oh. I have a steeper hill to climb than just that, huh?"

"O.K. Good bye for now."

In her former life Sara would have given up. The judge hadn't been impressed. What would it take? Sara envisioned a long hard road ahead of her.

"Marie Gonzales? Bill McCutcheon."

"You don't have to be surprised. I wanted you to dig up information on a Brent Jones who is now a prisoner at Rikers. I particularly want to know his medical records. I don't know how you're going to do it either. Just get him to sign a release or something."

"Thank you. And I need the report in a couple of days."

"Yes, I know you already have a heavy caseload. I'm just asking for a little extra out of you. Can you do it?"

The judge sat back in his chair and looked up at the crystal light fixture in the middle of the room. He remembered a time when a light bulb was the only light in his life.

"Bill, I'm gone."

"Because Sara's having problems?"

Bill and Dorothy McCutcheon were separating in 2007.

"Bill, that's only part of it."

"What else?"

"Bill, you've never grown up. When you were younger, you idolized Randall Smith, some blues artist you didn't even know, as if he were a god. I got the feeling that his words became your words and then the words between us. I didn't get to know Bill McCutcheon. I got to know some fan of a rock star. Then when you left him behind, you turned to sports. Every game was a big game. You had to watch every single damn game there was. When did we have a chance to talk? Never. Bill, I'm not really leaving you because I never was with you."

"Honey, how can you say these things? I liked Smith's music, yes, but his words, my words? I don't understand what you're saying. Are you saying I didn't have a life? I somehow managed to become a highly successful defense lawyer with a beautiful daughter who needs you."

"Save it Bill. It's too late. You can't hold me back. Bill, my mind is made up."

"OK.....all right. When are you leaving?"

"Heading out right now Bill. I'm taking the Jaguar. I have an apartment in Manhattan."

"We'll have to see each other to do the paperwork and all."

"You'll be getting a call from my lawyer. Good bye, Bill."

And Dorothy was gone.

Maybe she was right. Maybe she knew what she was talking about when she said their words came straight out of the mouth of Randall Smith because now Bill felt like he had half his heart out on the road in a car and the other half somewhere up on a stage in who knows where? The only brightness in his life came from a chandelier that would have still shown even if the world ended. And the world had ended.

The Lodge crew was in the van and heading to work. It was just another day. Once at the worksite, Sara got ready and went into Betty's room.

"Hi Sara. How's it going?"
"Good."

For once Sara did not have to lie. Things had been good lately, and they were good in the way Betty would have thought as good. Sara hadn't seen Bain in over a week. She hadn't used drugs, drank alcohol, or had sex in the same amount of time.

"How's your good behavior?" asked Betty.
"I've been pretty good," replied Sara.

"How's your Lodge doing? Isn't that what you call it? Your Lodge?"

"Yes. Well, our Lodge, not mine. We're a Fairweather Model of recovery."

"Recovery? Recovery from what?"

"Recovery from just about everything that comes with mental illness," said Sara.

She surprised herself that she could be so honest.

"Oh dear." Betty looked startled. Then she composed herself and said, "At least you're on the right track now. I don't want to know any more about your past life. I just need to see you getting better and better."

To Sara this was a huge challenge. How could she just block out her past as if it never happened? Maybe she only had to do this with Betty and possibly a few others. She could still talk about things with Jim, her friend at the Lodge.

"Yes. I've changed for the better. You couldn't believe what I was like before."

Betty could imagine though. She had a pretty good idea about issues with recovery due to a nephew's problems she had witnessed. However, she wouldn't tell this to Sara. She wanted Sara to think that her past was a disconnect with anything now or in the future. She wanted Sara to be a pleasant young lady. Sara, on the other hand, didn't know up from down. That was just the way Betty liked it. Made her easier to mold.

"Well, have a great day, Sara," said Betty and she grabbed her coat and purse and left.

For one of the first times Sara confronted herself with the question, *am I really the Virgin Mary, and if not, did I at least see an angel?* This was something that had been kept in her soul as mostly a secret except with disclosures to a few people including her father. Sara wanted to believe that she had witnessed God. She had to admit she hadn't lived the typical Christian life, but did that mean she wasn't a believer? The times she asserted herself as the Virgin Mary silently in her mind as she was bombarded with intrusive voices, voices that tried to undo her, were times that now made her shudder. The meds she was on now took care of the voices for the most part. Should she just forget the angel, the Virgin Mary stuff, that her father wouldn't allow her? In short, what was the truth? *I've been to AA meetings. I know if I'm going to get well, get respectable, and recover, then I'm going to need to be honest.* Then it hit Sara like a hammer, she'd have to confess. *Jesus, I know I'm not the Virgin Mary. I'm very sorry. It seemed like the right thing to do. You sent me an angel…I just didn't know. Please let me be Sara McCutcheon. I surrender to you, Lord. Please show me the way.* And Sara was done, done with her vacuuming, and done with being self-deluded. Rather, she was starting a life of honesty. Her heart was the mustard seed that Christ had mentioned in the Bible. She was all set to go. Only Bill McCutcheon knew how far she had come, and how far she had to go.

9

"Someone has played a cruel trick on you, Sara."

Bill wondered if he should be so up front, but Sara hadn't exactly been an angel. Bill's sense of justice required a price that Sara had to pay, if not to him, then society.

"Bain loves me and would do no such thing," quickly returned Sara who wasn't going to pay any price that Bill had set.

They stopped eating, and they both glanced up at the ceiling of the house where they had had Sunday dinners for nearly a quarter of a century.

"Do you really think God believes you are the Virgin Mary?" Bill thought that maybe that was too direct.

"I gave that up," said Sara proudly.

"You gave up your belief in God?"

"I didn't say that. I said that I gave up my belief that I was the Virgin Mary."

Bill paused. He thought long and hard before he said another word. Then he said, "That's good news and bad news." He sensitively looked at Sara to see what affect his words would have on her. She looked dumbfounded.

"What?"

Bill saw his chance. "When you believed you were the Virgin Mary, at least you were traveling with God."

"And what am I doing now?

"You're being Sara McCutcheon."

Sara's eyes got big. "Does that mean I'm not God's? Bill, you are really confusing me."

Bill had an appreciation for all the confusion treatment of a mental illness could bring up.

He thought a moment then said, "Sara, God loves you. I believe that. However, there are times where you weren't so nice…to me, and to the others."

"Bill this is too much. Can we stop talking now?"

Bill knew enough to back off. In a vague sort of way, he knew what kind of pressure he was putting on Sara, but from Sara's standpoint the judge didn't have a clue. To Sara, Bill was being a raging asshole.

Who does he think he is?

Bill thought back to the time Sara brought home her graded report card in 7th grade.

"Daddy, I got all "A's".
"Every single class?"
"Yes."
"Not even a "B" in one?"
"No. All "A's".
"That's my girl!"

I can't bear seeing her like this, no self-confidence, no grace, …no love.

Who the fuck does he think he is? Does he think he walks on water?

It was a good thing they kept their silence.

"Hello, this is Sara." Sara was at the Washington Lodge. It was about noon.

"Sara, it's Bain."
"Oh."
"Is that the way to greet your old buddy?"
"Bain, what do you want?"
"I haven't seen you in a couple of weeks. I'd like to see you."
"Bain, I'm busy."
"You're gonna let your old man tell you what to do, huh."

"That's not how it is. I'm making some changes for myself."

"You're becoming a goody-two-shoes."

"Bain, goodbye."

Only Bain could accuse me of being a sap. I'm still cool. I've always been cool. And I always will be cool.

"Sara?"

Sara looked over her shoulder. It was Jim.

"Hi, Jim."

"Sara, I kind of heard some of your phone conversation."

"You did?"

"Not much is private at the Washington."

"That's for sure."

"Sara, I just want to say that I think you're making the right decision. From all I know about Bain he's no good for you."

"Jim, you've always been in my corner for me, and I appreciate it. Maybe some day I'll do you a favor."

"Sara, you already have. Just seeing you making it now in the Lodge and everything. It's great."

"Thanks a lot Jim." \

Sara hugged Jim.

"It's about time for work, isn't it?"

That night at work, Sara could hardly wait to talk to Betty. Sara was so proud that she had given Bain the boot. However, when Sara, with vacuum in hand, entered the room, there was no Betty.

That's weird. She's probably sick. However, Betty was not there all week. Sara felt deprived. *I wonder what's up. Who can I ask about Betty?* The next week Sara went to the bulletin board which posted information on employees. That's when she saw it. Betty had been transferred to Chicago. *My God. Who can I lean on now?*

During the van ride home Sara was silent as snow. The others cast glances at her, but she stared straight ahead.

When they got out of the van in front of the Lodge, Millie took a jab at Sara.

"What's the matter, Sara, cat got your tongue?"

"Millie, I think it would be a whole lot more appropriate if you just shut up."

It could have been an incident, one that would have to go in front of the Lodge, but Millie decided she wouldn't make it a Lodge issue. This was personal and she'd handle it her way.

"Hello, Bill. It's Scott Jensen. Say, I'm here at my office with Maria Gonzales. We've been talking about Brent Jones."

"What's going on with that?"

"Bill, we were out to Rikers to see him. He's been highly responsive to the meds. We also learned that he had been on a six-month waiting list to see a psychiatrist. Plus, no priors, so I'm going to go along with you on him."

"Is he charged with any crime?"

"Creating a public disturbance."

"Not aggravated assault. We're lucky there."

"Turns out he has loving parents. I talked to them. They are very concerned."

"That helps. He'll have support."

"He's actually not a bad kid when he's on medication."

"Makes all the difference in the world."

"So, we'll be bringing him over next Monday to meet you for initiation into Mental Health Court."

"Scott, I know this is a tough one, but I think we're doing the right thing."

When the judge rode the train home that night he used his phone to call a psychologist who Molly had recommended through a friend.

"Hello, Miss Seneca's office."

"I'd like to speak to Miss Seneca."

"She's with a client. Can I help you?"

"It's my daughter. She's 23. I'd like her to see Miss Seneca."
"Does she have insurance?"
"She'll be under my policy."
"Good, we'll see her in two weeks on June 21 at 2 PM."
"She'll be there. Thank you."

As Sara entered the building in the Upper East Side of Manhattan, she had few expectations. She was still trying to turn her life around so she was glad that her father had arranged for her to meet with a therapist, but she found herself facing a boredom, a letdown from her fast-paced lifestyle she had had with Bain. Recovery was fine, but it sure was dull right now. Yet, she had made her decision; she was going straight.

She rode the elevator up to the third floor and followed the signs to room 321, Clara Seneca, Psychologist, MD – Art Therapy.

What's this? Art Therapy? Bill didn't tell me about this.

She entered the waiting room.

"Hello," said the receptionist, "You must be Sara McCutcheon."
"Yes. Yes I am."
"Ms. Seneca is just finishing with a client. Won't you have a seat?"

The way the receptionist said it, it felt a bit familiar, but Sara didn't object. In a minute or so, a young man emerged from what was Ms. Seneca's office. Then, a middle-aged woman appeared, who Sara surmised was Ms. Seneca. The greeting was very professional but warm. She extended her hand, and Sara, hers, and they shook.

Once in the room, Sara was impressed by the paintings on the wall.

"Who's the artist," asked Sara.

"Some are mine, and some are my students."

"I like the one of the unicorn."

"That was done by the man you just saw leaving."

"Really? Nice."

Clara told Sara to sit and pointed to an oversized lazy-boy in one of the corners of the blue room. Clara took a seat at her large oak desk.

"So Sara, tell me a little about yourself."

"What do you mean?"

"Anything you want. It's up to you."

"Nothing really comes to mind…"

"Come on Sara. Just one thing."

"I like the unicorn."

"Besides that. You already said that."

Sara realizing that she was at a therapist's off ice after all, seeking help, said the thing that had been on her mind for over five years.

"Some people think I'm the Virgin Mary."

"Really? That's interesting. How do you know they think you're Mary?"

"They tell me."

"Do they actually say it?"

"No. God no. They do it in more subtle ways."

"Like what?"

"Yesterday, I was at Jamieson's buying a candy bar…"

"You eat candy?"

"Let me tell the story please. Anyway, when I paid at the register, the clerk asked me if I wanted my change and winked."

"Yeah?"

"Don't you get it? She was asking me if I wanted to be changed from Sara McCutcheon to the Virgin Mary."

"How do you know she wasn't just talking about the change from your bill?"

"Oh you're worse than my dad."

"Speaking of your dad, how are you getting along with him?"

"Bill's all right."

"Don't you call him 'Dad'?"

"What do you want to know?"

"Well, Bill tells me you're doing well."

"I am doing fine."

"Back to this thing about the Virgin Mary - I don't believe you are."

For the first time since meeting Sara felt a little anxious. She really felt like she was on the hot seat. Ever since the day she had the spiritual revelation on the playing field at school, she had felt under attack. To her it felt like an attack on God. Most of the time she just let it go by, but she expected better from a doctor/psychologist. She wasn't sure how to respond. She did feel she wanted the doctor's help, but on the other hand the doctor seemed to choose to stick an invisible knife into her heart. Sara had been O.K. working on giving up the delusion on her own terms, but it was hurtful when someone else jumped on the bandwagon. It felt sacrilegious – a denial of a gift God had provided her.

"What makes you think I'm not?"

"You're Sara McCutcheon. You can't be anyone else."

"Who made that rule?"

That dumbfounded Ms. Seneca, but she chose to keep her composure because she sensed that Sara was really not O.K. If she gave in to Sara, Sara could spin out of control into the downward spiral she had seen so many persons with mental illness fall into.

"It's a rule because it is a fact. You can't change facts."

"I can."

"You see Sara, that's why you're here."

"Because I can change facts?"

"No. Because you cannot, and you don't know it."

Ms. Seneca realized she was getting combative, and this wouldn't be fruitful. With some of her patients she worked to get them to fight. She understood that with Sara this was no problem.

"Sara, I want you to draw me a picture." She handed Sara a clipboard with paper and some crayons.

"A picture?! A picture of what?"

"The Virgin Mary."

Sara laughed. "Are you serious?"

"Just go ahead and draw her."

So Sara acquiesced and drew a quick sketch of a woman wearing a shawl over her head. She showed it to Ms. Seneca.

"It doesn't look anything like you," said the therapist with questioning eyes, "but that's O.K. For our purposes, that's O.K."

Ms. Seneca then moved a garbage can to the center of the floor and produced a book of matches.

"Go ahead, Sara. Burn it."

"What?!"

"Do as I tell you."

So Sara struck a match, lit the paper on fire, and dropped it into the can.

"Are you satisfied?" asked Sara.

"Do you know why I had you do that?"

"Not really."

"You've got to burn through your delusions, Sara."

Sara felt very uncomfortable. "Why are we doing that?" asked Sara. "I like being the Virgin Mary."

"Sara, we're going to stop for today. I want you to go to work this afternoon and think of anything but being the Virgin Mary."

"I have to?"

"Sara, it's killing you."

Bill finally met Brent Jones. Gonzalez and Jensen brought him to the Mental Health Court to present his recovery plan.

"Hi, Brent. It's nice to meet you," said Bill after they entered his chambers.

"Judge McCutcheon, I sure appreciate this opportunity."

"I worked hard to get you here. I hope you put the opportunity to good use."

"I will, Judge. I will. I promise."

"You've got a lot of people pulling for you. I hope that's a good thing. It does increase the pressure, but sometimes stress is beneficial."

"Whatever you say, Judge."

"Brent, I don't just want a 'yes' man. You have to level with me. Do you think you can handle the stress?"

Ms. Gonzalez stepped in on that.

"Judge, I don't think you should be so hard of Brent. He just barely got out of jail."

Jones appeared to bristle at that.

"I can handle it. The judge isn't being rough on me."

Judge McCutcheon quickly replied, "Well let's get down to work."

That afternoon, Louis Chang, the Korean-American, had one of his check-in sessions with the Mental Health Court. His case worker, Lenny Barnes, was with him. When it was his turn, Chang and Barnes approached the bench where Judge McCutcheon presided.

"So, Louis how have you been?" asked the judge as he extended his hand and the two men shook.

"I think I've been good. I've been taking my meds, going to my 12-step group, and I have a couple leads on jobs."

"Oh yeah? What kind of work are you looking for?"

"Software design -what I do."

"Let's see. You've been out of work over two years. Is that right?"

"Yes."

"And you've been in Mental Health Court three months. Already your life is looking up. I'm proud of you."

"Thank you, Judge." He put his hands in his pockets and shrugged. His face beamed. "I just needed someone to give me a chance."

"You're earning my trust Mr. Chang."

"Judge, thank you."

"I'll see you in two weeks. Maybe you'll have good news for me then too."

One night when the Washington Lodge Crew got home, and they began to head off to their rooms, Millie started shouting.

"My gold watch is gone. Somebody stole my gold watch out of my bedroom. We've got to search the house from top to bottom. First, we'll check bedrooms."

When they got to Sara's room, Millie gave Sara the evil eye and said, "We've checked all the rooms Sara. I hope it's not in yours."

Upon entering the room all eyes went to the dresser on which lay a gold watch. They gasped.

Millie was the first to speak. "Yep. Just what I expected. Sara's the thief."

Sara just stood there in disbelief.

"I'm going to file a report with the police," said Millie.

The next day the Lodge had a meeting. Millie presided.

"I'm sorry it had to come to this," said Millie, "but we need to have a vote to kick you out of the Lodge."

"Don't I get a chance to defend myself," exclaimed Sara. "I didn't do it."

"How do you explain the watch lying on top of your dresser?"

"I'm being framed." Sara looked shocked. "I think it's you, Millie."

"Oh my God. Did you guys hear that? She's trying to blame me. I think we should take a vote right now," said Millie.

"Wait a minute," pleaded Jim, "all we have is circumstantial evidence."

"And the circumstances all point to Sara. Let's vote," demanded Millie. "All those in favor of terminating Sara as a Lodgemate, raise your hand."

Everybody except Jim and Sara raised their hands.

"That does it Sara. Be out within 24 hours."

10

Sara tried calling her dad at home the next day. He wasn't there so she left a message.

The judge was actually experiencing a severe setback in the Mental Health Court. He looked at the breaking news on his computer screen.

A young man with an assault rifle killed four people and injured six more at a McDonald's restaurant at mid-day in Manhattan before being killed by police. He has been identified as Brent Jones, 26.

The report went on but McCutcheon couldn't watch anymore.

"Molly," said the judge, "something's come up. Cancel my appointments. I'm going home."
"What is it Bill?"
"Molly, I think it's best not to get into it."
"Bill, you always tell me everything."
"Molly. Brent Jones is dead. He went on a shooting spree."
"My God, Bill. Yes. Go home. Bill, it's not your fault."

When Bill got home he had a message from Sara on the phone. He did not feel like talking to Sara right now. He wasn't there five minutes and the phone rang.

"Dad, it's me Sara."
"Sara, it's not a good time."
"Dad, I'm kicked out of the Lodge for stealing. I need to come home."

"Sara, not now."

"What? What are you saying?"

"Sara, you can't come here."

"Dad. I didn't do it. I swear…"

"Sara, don't make it difficult."

"But Dad. I'm coming there. I will…"

"Sara, I'll have you arrested for trespassing."

"Dad. Where will I go?"

"Bain, this is Sara."

"Sara who?" Click.

"Sara, your time is up. You out of here."

Millie stood there marking time with her gold watch.

"Millie, you know and I know I didn't do it. Wherever I end up, this isn't through."

With duffel bag in hand holding a couple days change of clothes, toiletries, a 30-day supply of meds, and a Bible, Sara walked out of the Long Island house that had been her Lodge for the past year. In her purse, she had her last paycheck for $750.00 and an entitlement check from the federal government for $1100.00 plus about $50 in cash.

She considered calling her mother. She decided to give that a try. However, Dorothy quickly negated any chance of Sara staying with her, telling Sara, "It's not my problem." Sara had been on the streets for a couple of weeks when she was 17, but that was more like running away from home. At that time, she had been too crazy to worry. Now she was in some middle ground between sanity and insanity. This time she had no desire to be on the streets, and she was scared and angry and depressed. *I have to go on.*

She felt a pull to go into Manhattan. That's where her father worked. That's where her mother lived. She'd look for a shelter.

Sara began to feel herself slipping. The first thing she felt were the trees. They were now puncturing holes in her soul. People's faces looked ugly. What had been beautiful and gentle became alien and threatening. It started so subtly, but Sara knew it would never stop. She had feared this moment her entire life – when what was precious became jaded. What had brought her happiness, now caused pain. She was defenseless. Everything was upside down. There was no getting off. God became something too immense for her mind. Her belief that she was the Virgin Mary had caused her to become unglued. Sara didn't know who or what she was. All she had was a faint light, a memory, and a fading hope. This was certainly something she could tell no one.

She took the Long Island Rail Road to Queens and a #7 to the public library at 5th & 42nd in Manhattan. She was able somewhat miraculously to put one foot ahead of the next. It was all instinct. Once inside the library she went to the service desk to ask about using a computer.

"You have to have a valid library card," said the staff worker.
"How do I do that?" asked Sara.
"You have to go online to download the application."
"If I need a card to use a computer, how can I use the computer to get a card?"
"Sorry. Can't help you."
Sara didn't know if the clerk was being impossible because the clerk didn't like Sara, or if everyone was treated that way. A gentleman who overheard the conversation leaned over.

"I'll log on, and you can get the application," he offered.

There still are some saints in the world.

"I'm just curious. What information are you trying to gather?" he asked.
"Trying to find a shelter."
"Are you…homeless?"
"Now I am."
"Tell me your story."
Sara related the events in her life that had led up to her current predicament. She was warmed by the apparent caring of a stranger. She didn't tell him about the Virgin Mary thing. She was trying to put that in God's hands.

"That's quite a story," he said. "Where are your parents?"
"My father is the judge of Mental Health Court."
"Really. What's his name?"
"Bill McCutcheon."
"Really. I know Bill. I'm on the City Council."
"Then maybe you can help me. My father won't talk to me."
"Really?"

The man stepped back a step, and smiled a weak grin.

"I'm afraid I can't get involved in a father-daughter dispute."
He turned and walked away.

Sara couldn't comprehend what had just happened. *Maybe he's biased against the Virgin Mary. After all I'm responsible for Jesus, and a lot of people are afraid of Jesus. He'll get his some day. 'I don't get involved in father-daughter disputes'. What a joke. Yeah Buddy, you're a joke.* Sara a woman with huge needs was just not getting them met.

She tried to focus her attention on the computer screen but was not able to concentrate. She had missed her morning dose of medication and did not have any medication on her. *I don't need medication. I don't need any homeless shelter either. I'm the Virgin Mary. I deserve a castle. Where's my castle?*

When Bill showered one morning a week after Jones's shooting rampage, and Sara's ejection from the Lodge, Bill noticed that there was a lot of hair in the drain. *It must be getting to me.* It wasn't vanity. It wasn't self-pity. It was more that Bill suddenly felt tired. *Maybe I'm depressed. Should I see a doctor? Then people would think I'm not fit for my job. Who cares? What about Sara though? She really needs me to be strong. I'll play it by ear.*

On his way to work he picked up the newspaper. It wasn't until he got on the subway that he saw the article tucked inside, **"JUDGE'S DAUGHTER HOMELESS"**.

The article was an interview with Sara about her homeless condition. Apparently, Sara had contacted the Times and given the story.

When the judge got to the office, he didn't have to say anything. He could tell that Molly knew.

"Bill, these are hard times for you. You have my shoulder to lean on if you need it."

"Thanks, Molly. That helps a lot."

He hadn't been in his chambers more than a moment when he got a call.

"Yes, Bill? This is Josh Seiling from the governor's office. What's this about your daughter being homeless?"

"Oh you saw the article," said Bill rather sheepishly.

"What's going on?"

"Sara and I are having our difficulties right now."

"We can't have that kind of publicity, Bill. We're Democrats. We're not supposed to have these kinds of problems."

"Josh, I'm under a lot of stress. With the Jones thing and Sara…"

"You sure guessed wrong on the Jones thing, Bill."

"Josh, it's a calculated risk…"

"The governor's not happy. Got to do better, Bill."

"Yeah."

"I need a commitment, Bill."

"O.K. You got it."

After he hung up, Bill got on the intercom with Molly.

"Molly, do I have anything pressing today? Anything that just can't wait?"

"No Bill. I suggest you take the rest of the day off."

"Is that an order?"

"Yes."

Instead of getting on the subway Bill walked up the street until he came to a small, nameless bar. He went inside and proceeded to get drunk. He didn't remember much when he woke up in his bed the next morning. All he knew is that he had a huge headache. *What day is it? Thursday. What time is it? 10:15.*

Then the phone rang. It was Molly worried about where he was.

"Molly, I got drunk last night."

"What?"

"I haven't been drunk since law school."

"Bill? Are you O.K.?"

"I'll be in, Molly. I'm coming in."

But Bill didn't make it in. He took one look in the mirror and said, "I can't make it."

"Molly, I won't be in after all."

"Bill, this really doesn't sound like you."

"There's just too much going on."

"What are you saying Bill?"

"I need some time to think things out."

"Bill, I hate to say this, but maybe you need help."

"Help? Yes, perhaps you're right."

"Hello, can I speak to Miss Seneca?"

"Ah, she's with a client right now."

"This is kinda urgent."

"Are you a client of hers?"

"Not really, but my daughter is. I'm Bill...Bill McCutcheon."

"You say it's urgent?"

"Yes. I'd like to see her right away."

"Well, she did have a cancellation at 3:00 today."

"Good. I'll take it. Thanks. Bye."

"Hello," said Bill poking his head in the door at the psychologist's office.

"You can come in," said the receptionist. "You must be Mr. McCutcheon."

"Yes. Yes I am."

"Go ahead in. Ms. Seneca has been waiting for you."

Bill looked at his watch. Three o'clock on the dot. He wondered if she had been waiting. He went in her office and was greeted with a handshake.

"Judge McCutcheon, how nice to meet you."

"Well thanks. It's nice to meet you too."

"But it is a little surprising."

"How so?"

"Sara never mentioned that you were having any difficulty."

"Oh...yeah...I suppose. I mean did you and Sara talk about me?"

"I can't go into detail, but, yes, your name did pop up, but only your name. We didn't discuss anything personal."

"I see."

"Have a seat."

She pointed to the lazy-boy. She sat at her oak desk.

"What can I do for you, Mr. McCutcheon?"

"Bill. I'm Bill to most people, even Sara."

Bill slipped off his coat. The weather outside this March day was unseasonably cold and required a coat.

"Ms. Seneca, I was hoping you could tell me."

"What?"

"I don't really know what is wrong with me, but I know something is."

"Well let's find a place to begin."

"My ex-wife says my word is no good. How about that?"

"Do you think your word is no good?"

"She suggests that my word is not even my own but rather the words of my boyhood idol Randall Smith."

"Oh, you liked Randall Smith?"

"Have you ever heard of him?"

"Of course."

"When I was young I couldn't get enough of him."

"And how about now?"

"Well I'm a grown man."

"You're not answering me. What is your relationship with Randall Smith now?"

"I was his lawyer back a few years."

"You represented him in court?"

"Yes. I got him off too."

"I bet he was thankful for that."

"I'm sure he was."

"But that doesn't answer my question. What is your relationship with Smith now?"

"I guess I don't really know."

"Has he just 'dropped' out of your life?"

"I wouldn't put it like that."

"How would you put it then?"

"In some ways, I've moved on."

"Do you really think you have? Or do you just 'think' you have."

Bill and Clara talked on for another 45 minutes. When they were done, Clara felt the two had established a working relationship; Bill felt like he had just revealed his deepest flaw, his inability to escape the shadow of his hero.

11

When Bill went to work on Friday, he saw Molly's look of apprehension on her face.

"Good morning Bill."

Molly was laying back waiting for some clue on how Bill was doing.

"Hi Molly. I guess you wonder how I'm doing."

"It's not like you Bill to miss work."

"I'm getting help, Molly."

"Do you want to talk about it?"

"It's all coming down to my word, Molly."

"What do you mean, Bill."

"Dorothy always said my word isn't good."

"What are you talking about, Bill? Your word has always been good."

"Dorothy said I 'borrowed' Randall Smith's words."

"Bill, I'll be damned if I know what you're talking about."

"It's just that how can I compete with Smith's words?"

"Bill, I'm having a hard time making any sense out of what you're saying."

"Yeah, I guess I'm getting weird."

"Yeah. Too weird."

Molly clenched her fist and gave an upper cut punch in the air.

"Go to work, Bill."

Bill went into his chambers, but he did not go to work. He was becoming overwhelmed with self-reproach. A black cloud was coming over his mind. *I can't do this. I'm a judge. They know I'm a fake. Randall Smith. All I ever did was follow him down the primrose path. Where is he now? Clara is right. He's dropped off the face of the map. Am I O.K.? No. No, I'm not. Maybe I should resign my position.* Bill went on like this for a period of about a half hour, then as quickly as the black cloud had descended, it lifted.

> "Molly, I'm O.K."
> "What's that, Bill?" said Molly over the intercom.
> "Never mind, Molly. Everything is fine."
> "Get back to work, Bill."
>
> "I want to talk to Ms. Seneca."
> "This is Sara McCutcheon."
> "Ms. Seneca, I want to come in."
> "You can bill my father's insurance."
> "O.K. See you this afternoon."
> Sara showed up for her appointment on time.
> Ms. Seneca greeted her, "Hi, Sara. You're looking well."

Only a therapist could have said Sara was looking well.

> "Well, I'm just trying to maintain."
> "How so?" said Clara motioning for Sara to take a seat.
> "I'm on the streets now you know."
> "What?! What about the Lodge?"
> "They kicked me out for stealing."
> "Oh yeah?" said the therapist with a sly smile.
> "But I didn't do it. I was framed by one of the others."
> "Is that so," said Ms. Seneca, not really indicating whether she believed Sara or not.
> "Yeah."
> "What about a place at your dad's?"

Clara didn't think it wise to divulge that Bill was now a client.

"He won't let me stay there either."

"So how long has it been?"

"About a week."

"Oh my God."

"It's not so bad. I found a place under a bridge…"

"Sara, this can't be. We've got to find you a place…"

"That's not why I came here. I want to know about what you think about me being the Virgin Mary."

"It's nonsense Sara. You're mentally ill."

"No. What do you really think? Look in my eyes. Tell me what you see?"

"A very pretty girl."

"Don't give me that B.S. What do you really see?"

"What am I supposed to see?"

"God." Sara was almost up out of her seat. "Can't you see my God?"

"Everyone is a child of God."

"Can't you see that I'm special? That I am indeed the Virgin Mary?"

"Truthfully? Sara, I can't."

"Then I'm wasting my time."

"Oh no, Sara. Talking to me is not wasting your time. I know your time is valuable."

"That's because I have a special place in God's kingdom."

"I think it's because you have a special place in your father's heart."

"Why'd you have to bring him up? He doesn't love me. He don't care."

Ms. Seneca still opted to not tell Sara about her dad's being under her care. It was coming at Ms. Seneca very fast. She balanced her intention to push Sara towards independence with Sara's need for support.

"If you don't need him then I won't bring him up. But I do know he loves you. He may not love you as the Virgin Mary. He loves you as his daughter,"

Sara had no response.

"Say, where did you get the idea that you were the Virgin Mary?"

Sara related the story in the schoolyard.

"Are you even Catholic?"

"No. Methodist."

"Very interesting that God has manifested Himself to you in the revelation of you as the Virgin Mary."

"Then you believe me?" asked Sara getting excited.

"Not so fast. I do believe in revelations that happen to some people. However, that doesn't mean you turn into a new person."

"Jesus began his ministry when a dove descended from heaven."

"Jesus was very unique. You're not like Jesus."

"I think I am."

"Sara? Are you celibate?"

"I haven't had sex in a month."

Ms. Seneca couldn't resist smirking.

"That doesn't make you a saint."

"What would make me a saint?"

"That's a loaded question. I think we will stop for now. We will continue this at our next session."

"That's it? We're done? I was just getting started."

"Sara, I've got another patient."

"Just answer me one last question."

"What is it Sara?"

"Will you pray for me?"

Sara walked back to her "home" under the bridge. People watched her as she climbed the embankment slid under a metal beam and lay down on the flat surface with the road a mere three feet above her. She had been going on adrenalin. She had a hard time quieting her mind. In fact, her mind was shooting about like a pinball machine. On the flip side, everything she did was slow and deliberate. She was 23 but looked to be 40. She had tried to wash up in a restaurant restroom, but she could only get so clean that way. What she did have was a guiding light, the same light she saw back in the schoolyard. It was the old lady. Had she been an angel? Sara thought so. But what did that get her? She wanted to share the light with others. And she wanted people to believe she was the Virgin Mary incarnate. This was her truth. But why had she ended up with Bain? He was about as religious as a skunk. Something told her that she had better begin to try to make sense to others.

Sara began to feel sleepy and she closed her eyes. Then they came. Footsteps. At first Sara thought she was hallucinating, but suddenly she felt a hand on her chest, then a knife on her throat.

"Don't try to scream," said the voice. "Just do as I say and nobody gets hurt."

Sara knew immediately what the situation was. She had heard of rape, but she just didn't think it would ever happen to her.

After it was over the man left. Sara had not even wanted to see his face. She had never been overpowered by anyone before. She felt so dark and so alone. Police? They'd never believe her. How were they going to believe a mentally ill homeless girl? Silently she sobbed. It was as though her last card had been beaten. Taken. Fear entered her heart. This was the worst. Absolute worst. Then nothing mattered anymore. Nothing significant was left. She burst out with a hideous laugh. *Wait. I still have my light. But a virgin? No. The Virgin Mary? No. But there's still a light. God is that you? Must be. Talk to me God. Please say something.* Silence. *Go to hell God. No that's not right. Where do I go from here? Bill always said in the words of Randall Smith,* "Sometimes there's no way but up."

In the next five minutes Sara found herself at a hotel payphone.

"Hello, I want to talk to Jim."

"I know it's late. I need…"

"Hello, Jim? It's Sara."

"Yeah, I'm homeless, but Jim? Jim? I just got raped."

"I'm not making this up. Jim? Jim? I need to see you."

"Grand Central? What time? 9:00 A.M.? I'll see you. What? I'll probably book a room at this hotel. I know I don't have much money, but I just can't… OK, OK. Tomorrow."

Then she walked over to the desk.

"I'd like a room."

"Do you have any money?" asked the hotel desk clerk.

"I didn't think you would give the room to me for free. Here. Here's $200. How much do you want?"

"That should cover it except the tax."

"You get your cut and the government gets theirs. I'm the one who can't win."

12

Bill was fumbling through his caseload on his PC. He now had 82 active defendants in the mental health court. It was Monday, April 2 2012. A little over a year had passed since Louis Chang, the first candidate, had come in front of him. Chang had progressed well. He now had a job in his field and was engaged to be married. Being the first must have brought him good luck. Not all the defendants had been so lucky. However, there was one that caused Bill great joy, his favorite, Willie Douglas, who had gone from a thief to a success. His story was the stuff of miracles.

Willie was shaky for the first few months. Then something in his character took hold. He got accepted in a Fairweather Program, the same organization Sara had participated in. Bill had facilitated the transition. Presto. Willie had a roof over his head and a job. He even had his own bedroom. He had been sober six months now.

Bill saw how Fairweather had created Willie's success, but the joy that came with that was tempered by the tragedy of Sara's life. Not only was Sara's story tragic, everyone knew about it too. The newspaper had had a running serial on Sara and Bill's life. Sara always found a journalist to give her an ear.

The fallout of such attention was more rebuke from the governor's office. They told Bill he had to get Sara off the streets. He just wondered how.

"Dorothy, it's Bill."
"Yes? I haven't forgotten your voice you know."
"Dorothy, it's about Sara."
"No surprise there. All of New York knows about Sara."

"It seems she's making a point. She's almost relishing her homeless situation. She even got a Lodgemate from her old Fairweather Lodge, a guy named Jim, to come out on the streets and join her."

"Brother."

"That's why I'm calling. We have got to end this charade."

"And what do you want from me, Bill?"

"Honey..."

"Honey!?"

"Dorothy, then. Dorothy I'd like to try again."

"Are you nuts, Bill?"

"We're Sara's parents. She's our only child. Dorothy, she needs us."

"What exactly are you proposing Bill?"

"I'd like to welcome you and Sara back home."

There was a long, long pause.

"Bill, you think we can go back? We can just go back seven years? Just like that?"

"Honey, I mean Dorothy, people do it all the time."

"Well, I'm not just anybody. I've got my life."

"What? Working temps? Watching T.V.?"

"But Bill..."

"Honey, we could rescue our daughter's life."

"Well..."

"Honey, you still love Sara, and for that matter I think you still love me."

"It's just this mental illness stuff. It's so weird."

"Doesn't have to be. When it all comes down to it, it's just a medical condition."

"Well..."

"Honey, we could still give Sara a life."

"I still love her. I think about you two a lot."

"Just say you'll consider it."

The seed was planted. Within a week Dorothy was back at the Tudor mansion in White Plains.

"Do you have any idea where Sara is?"

Bill and Dorothy were seated at the dining room table. Dorothy's suitcases were still by the front door.

"Somewhere in Manhattan," said Bill.

"Just like you Bill…"

"Honey don't get started on me. No one cares more than I do about Sara's well-being."

"Bill, she thinks she's the goddamn Virgin Mary."

"Honey. Honey? It's a little more complex than that."

"Why can't she just be our little girl?"

"It's rebellion. She's going through a very difficult time."

"I think it's brain chemistry."

"That's certainly part of it."

Bill leaned back in his chair.

"Honey, would you like a cup of tea?"

"With honey. You know the way I like it."

Bill disappeared into the kitchen for a couple of minutes as he poured the water from the sink, got out two tea bags, and put it all in the microwave. Then he came back into the dining room.

"Bill, what is she doing for money?"

"I've been sending her money through a Clara Seneca who is a psychologist."

"Oh."

"You don't sound happy."

"How's she going to become independent?"

"We have to make sure she stays alive first."

"Sara, how much money do we have?" asked Jim.

"Jim don't worry. We have enough."

Sara and Jim were in "The Grounder You Get" coffee shop just a couple of blocks from Central Park. Jim had left the Washington Lodge to join Sara on the streets several months ago. Sara had been on the streets three months previous to that.

"You don't get your SSI check until the 3rd. That's a week away."

"My dad will send a check to my therapist's office sometime in the next few days."

"Maybe we should go over there."

"What the hell. Why are you so worried about money?"

"I like to eat. Food is good."

"And what's wrong with the free meals we get?"

"It just makes me feel poor."

"Baby, we are poor."

"Just watch the way you call me baby."

"Jim, what is with you today?"

"Look, I'm mentally ill. And so are you."

"What'd you call me?"

"Sara, the whole reason our life is this way is because we both have a mental illness."

"I chose this life."

"Sara, you're homeless because you got kicked out of the Lodge for something you didn't do and you had no place to go."

"Don't be so logical. I'm gonna call you Mr. Logic."

"Sara, I love you, but…"

"Hold it right there. Did you just say what I thought you said?"

"Yes. Yes, I did. And I meant it."

"I don't use the word so loosely."

"Sara?"

"Yes?"

"Let's pull a job."

"What the hell are you talking about?"

"Get some money."

"Jim? You? I thought I left that behind when I got rid of Bain."

"Maybe I'm vying for that position in your heart that he filled."

"Jim, I don't want you to…"

"Sara. For me? Won't you do it for me?"

"Oh my God. Jim, what do you want to do? A bank robbery?"

"No. Nothing like that. Something with a little class."

"I got it."

"I'm all ears."

"I go strut my stuff, and like a guy will come up and proposition me, and then like I take his money, but I have to use the bathroom in the hotel, and meanwhile you come up and interrupt him while I'm in the women's room, and I duck out with the money."

"Go on. That'll never work."

"You got any other ideas?"

"O.K., ok. I'm game."

"Bill, if there was just a way to get her back to the house."

"Our house?"

"Oh, it's our house. I thought it was your house."

"C'mon honey. We shouldn't be fighting. We have a daughter to save."

"Are we really trying to save her or just give her a life?"

"You're trying to make something simple that's very complex."

"What exactly do you mean by 'save her'"?

"It's kind of Biblical, isn't it?"

"You mean through Jesus?"

"Well…"

"I think it's the ideas put in your head by your hero."

"Randall Smith?"

"The very same."

"Oh honey. I've forgotten him."

"Bullshit. You are a walking disciple of your blues artist friend."

"How can you say that? I'm a fuckin' Christian."

"How can you put those two words in the same sentence?"

"Calm down. Calm down."

"I will be calm when you admit that you never gave Sara and me a life."

"What are you accusing me of?"

"You were always goody-two-shoes. Too good for us."

"I don't have to hear this."

"Go ahead. Run away. Just like you always did. When the going got tough you turned and ran. Every goddamn time."

"O.K. O.K. I'm not running now. Not this time. I gave you and Sara a decent middle-class life. We had respect in the community. We have a nice house. What more is there?"

"It's just that...just that you had something in your heart for Randall Smith and you had something for me...at least when we started out. But, and that's a big but, you never conveyed that to Sara. Sara never got your Randall Smith feeling in her heart."

"Wow."

"Can't you see? She missed the boat."

"Don't you think she has a mental illness?"

"Because when she searched her insides, she came up empty."

"Sounds like you're trying to hold me accountable for Sara's mental health."

"Aren't you supposed to be accountable?"

"For Sara's life?"

"What of your values? The values Randall Smith invoked that you so dearly clung to at one time?"

"I still have my values."

"And you've got to help Sara develop hers."

"Now we're on the same page. There's nothing more that I would like to see in Sara than some values. But she's got to arrive at those herself."

"It's up to us to help her. We're her parents."

"Don't you think it's a little late in the game for that?"

"Some people are having children in their 50's even 60's. No, it's never too late."

Bill was seated at his desk when Molly buzzed him.

"It's Sara on the phone," said Molly.

"Put her on."

"Dad, I'm in jail."

"What? What happened?"

"It was just a scam. Jim, my friend from the Washington and I were just trying to make a little money on the side."

"What'd you do?"

"I got a man to proposition me. Then we were going to run with the money. But there was a cop there, and, well, that's about it."

"Who was this man?"

"Turns out he's on the governor's staff. You might know him. He's a clerk for Joshua Seiling."

"My God." Bill sat back not knowing whether to laugh or to cry. Life was a circle game.

"Bill, Scott Jenson here."

"Now why was I expecting your call?"

"Hold on. Just a moment. I'm trying to be helpful."

"You're calling about Sara, right?"

"Yes. Yes, I am. But I'm not going to say what you expect me to say."

Bill adjusted himself in his chair.

Jensen went on, "I think Sara is a good candidate for the Mental Health Court."

"What?! Scott is this you?"

"I know. I know. It's out of character for me."

"But Scott. I can't judge my own daughter."

"That's easy. Recuse yourself from the case. There's any one of a dozen or so judges we could have sit in."

"Well…"

"Bill, I want to see you successful with Sara. I know how much you care and everything. Maybe this time will be the game-breaker. Maybe Sara will get a life."

"Scott, she thinks she's the Virgin Mary."

"Careful Bill. Don't tell that to everybody."

"I know. I've just never seen someone lose their whole identity before."

"Lot of people have changed for the better with your help and the Mental Health Court. I don't see why Sara can't too."

"Dorothy and I…"

"What? Dorothy's back in the picture?"

"Yes. She's moved back into the house. We're making a play to save Sara."

"I'm not sure about 'saving' her. But I wish you good luck."

"So, you think I can get Sara into the Mental Health Court? I'll have to think about that a while. But, hey, thanks for the call."

13

"Bill? Are you ready?" asked Molly. "You have a very important caller on the line."

"Who would that be?"

"Your hero, Randall Smith."

"You're kidding. Tell me you're kidding."

"No, I'm not Bill. Don't keep Mr. Smith waiting."

"Hello? This is Bill McCutcheon."

"Randall Smith."

"Mr. Smith!"

"Randall."

"Randall! To what do I owe this honor?"

"I'll get right to the point. I'm writing a book. A book about my life. Some of the highlights. I'm not really writing it myself, you see. I'm asking people who knew me to write short stories."

"I'd love to…but don't you have a publicist who can…"

"Let me finish. I want to ask you if you'd be able to write a story about the court case where you defended me and won."

"Randall, it'd be my pleasure."

"You think you'd do that for me?"

"Just tell me when you need it by."

"Oh, I haven't set the time frame yet. Maybe a couple of months."

"Sure. Sure, Randall. I could do that. How many words?"

"Hadn't thought about it exactly. Whatever it takes. Oh, say 1000."

"Yeah, I could do that. You're putting together a book, huh?"

"For progeny. You know. Speaking of progeny, how's the little girl, what was her name again?"

"Sara. She's not such a little girl now."

"Is she coming into herself?"

"I'm sorry?"

"Is she finding herself?"

"Oh sure. She's coming around."

"What's she doing with her time?"

"Say Randall, I know you're a busy man. You don't have time to hear about my life. I'll get that article to you."

"No not at all. You know I'll be in New York in a couple of weeks. I'll swing by."

"What? I mean sure. I'm in Manhattan."

"I know. I hunted you down to get your number. We'll go out to lunch and bring Mary."

"Sara. It's Sara."

"Right. Be talking to you."

"Take care Randall."

Bill sat back. On the one hand, it would be great to see Randall. On the other, how was he going to handle Sara? The social pressure of being out in public with Randall Smith would be quite a challenge. Bill hadn't seen Sara for four months. With Dorothy coming back into the picture, a lot of things were up in the air. Smith would have his sensors up. He always did. He'd know if something wasn't right. Bill always wanted to be perfect around Smith. It was like a private in front of a general. Could he make an excuse and not bring Sara? No, Smith would smell that out.

"Molly, bring me a cup of coffee…the big mug…black."

"O.K. Sara. My name is Maria Gonzalez. I've been appointed to be your attorney."

The two of them sat in a room at Rikers prison.

"What about Jim?"

"We'll talk about him too. But you've got to worry about yourself."

"We got into this together, and we'll get out of it together."

"Well, let me tell you what's in the works."

"Anything to get me out of here."

"Sara, there's a lot of paperwork and interviews, but in the end, we'll be setting you up for Mental Health Court."

"No frickin' way. Are you nuts? Go to Bill's home ground?"

"Sara, why do you want to fight your father?"

"Do I have to write you a letter? Don't you get it? Fire and gasoline don't mix."

"Now just a second. First off, it won't be your father as judge. Number two, you're in hot water. You should take all the help you can get."

"I won't be part of it unless Jim goes too. I go nowhere without Jim."

"Well that wasn't in the plan…"

"Jim was the one who met me at my level. He came out and hung with me on the streets."

"Does he have a mental illness?"

"Of course. He's in the Lodge just like I was."

"So, that might be a possibility."

Gonzalez stood up. She took a careful read of Sara, then left.

Shortly she was on the phone to Jensen, the prosecutor.

"So, Scott, Sara McCutcheon won't go for Mental Health Court unless her friend Jim Nielsen gets on board too."

"Oh. This is Maria Gonzalez. I'm talking about getting Sara and her friend into Bill's court."

"Yes, I know Bill won't be the judge. Has a judge been appointed yet?"

"I'm moving too fast?"

"O.K. All right. It's just that I hate to see any of my clients in jail any longer than they have to be. What are we looking at? A week? A month?"

"I can go ahead with the paperwork on both of them?"

"Thanks Scott. Thanks so much."

Bill and Dorothy were adjusting with living together again. They ate together but didn't share a bedroom.

"So, you guys down at the courthouse are going to bring Sara and her friend into the fold?" said Dorothy.

"That's the plan," replied Bill.

"And what's this about you and Sara having lunch with Randall Smith?"

"His idea."

"Bill, do you ever think I might want to be involved in some of this planning?"

"Didn't know you were interested."

"Damn you Bill. Do you think I moved back to the house because…well just because? She happens to be my daughter too. I think I should be consulted on these things."

"Do you want to come with when we see Randall?"

"I don't know. What do you think?"

"Honey? You tell me you want a voice then you don't use it."

"O.K. Sure. I'll have lunch with Randall. We'll bring Jim too?"

"I'd like to make reservations on October 6th for two o'clock for five."

Molly was doing extra duty.

"We don't usually take reservations that far out."

"It's an important person."

"So? And in whose name are these for?"

"Randall Smith." Molly took delight in the opportunity to drop a name. "And that's thee Randall Smith."

"The blues player?"

"The very one."

"Well, we've had important guests, Senator Thomas, even the mayor…"

"Don't you have a patio connected to the main restaurant?"

"Yes. I can arrange for a table on the patio if you'd like."

"We'd like the whole patio."

"Well. That's quite unusual."

"Randall Smith is an unusual man."

"I see. For the right price, I guess…"

"The price is not a factor."

"O.K. then. We'll look forward to seeing you on October 6th at 2 P.M. Could be cold."

"Just be sure he doesn't get hounded for autographs."

"Yeah. Yeah, sure."

The restaurant, *The New Yorker*, was a steakhouse. It was located in Greenwich Village, a place where Smith might be recognized, but where the people might also be cool enough not to make a fuss. Molly was grateful she never had to worry about someone wanting her autograph. Oh, she once had the yearning to be an actress on Broadway or the movies, but she had given that up at age 14 when her mother died and she had to raise herself and her younger brother. She had never told Bill about this hardship, and Bill had always shied away from probing her with questions. But both of them were familiar with the power of the limelight. Molly had been diverted by necessity, and Bill had lived vicariously through his hero, Randall Smith. Although the last year or so, Bill had found himself getting a lot more publicity than he really wanted.

"Bill? Josh Seiling, the governor's office."
Bill knew what the subject was before the conversation went any further, but he laid back.
"Oh, hi Josh."
"Bill, I don't have to tell you, the governor is not pleased about this situation with your daughter."
The last thing Bill wanted was pressure put on Sara. She was living with the burden of thinking she was the Virgin Mary. All that that entailed was only known by Sara, even though Bill had a few guesses.

"I'm not sure what to say Josh. Your man was involved too."
"How'd you know that?"
"A little birdie told me."
"Sara?"

"It takes two to Tango, Josh. If your man hadn't been there…"

"Now what's going to happen?"

"We're actually grooming Sara and her friend for Mental Health Court."

"You can't be serious. With you as judge?"

"I'm going to recuse myself."

"What kind of circus are you trying to run?"

"And I have the same question for you. Look, I have a daughter I'm trying to save, and I hope you can appreciate that."

"I don't know, Bill. I just don't know. The way you're going about things. But…even the governor can bend a little in certain circumstances. The best to you, Bill."

"Molly? Can you get Maria Gonzales on the line?"

At Rikers, a guard leaned into the cell where Jim was.

"You seem like a pretty clean-cut kid."

"I don't know."

"Did that girlfriend of yours get you in this trouble?"

"Wait a minute. I'm just as guilty as she is."

"Sometimes I know that certain girls try to get nice boys in trouble."

"I'm not a boy, and I take full responsibility for my actions."

"Now why do you want to get yourself in more trouble?"

"They say love is a wonderful thing when it goes both ways for better or worse."

"What would a young punk like you know about love?"

"I'm learning a little bit every day and it ain't from you."

"You're kind of sassy for someone who's in trouble with the law."

"Well you haven't shown me much respect."

"Respect? You expect that?"

"Every human being deserves respect."

"In my generation, you earned it."

14

Bill was at an appointment with Ms. Seneca, the psychologist. This was his fifth session. He felt like she was helping. He had been able to get back on his feet at work. The time he got drunk was the only time he got drunk. However, he wanted to get a handle on his relationship with Sara and his relationship with Dorothy.

"So, Bill, I want to go back to something you said in an earlier session. You told me Dorothy said your words were really Randall Smith's words, that she didn't really know you. Do you think that's true?"

"Well, at first it floored me. I know I clung to Randall's words as a youth, but I've gone out and made my own life. I have my own identity."

"Do you?"

"What are you asking me? I'm not Randall's twin or something. I have a life if that's what you mean."

"From whom did you get this life?"

"My parents I guess."

"Bill, I have a real sense that you adopted Smith's ideas as your own, and you're still living them out to this day."

"I believed in his message if that's what you mean. What are you driving at?"

"I think Bill McCutcheon was lost somewhere back as a teenager."

"What?!"

"You identified so strongly with this charismatic personality that you didn't learn to be yourself."

"Oh, I don't know…"

"When was the last time you had a good cry?"

"You're asking me all these questions."

"When was it Bill? Ten years ago? Twenty years?"

"Probably when I last listened to Smith's *Bluewaters* record. It always made me cry."

"Hah! And you don't think Smith runs your life?"

"I like him. But runs my life? Isn't that a little extreme?"

"I think your relationship with Smith was extreme. You lost your balance."

"What's the difference if some guy worships some baseball player?"

"Maybe there is no difference. Doesn't make it right. Can't you see that Sara and Dorothy needed more out of you than your loyalty to some rock musician?"

"Blues artist."

"Don't spilt hairs with me Bill. This is something you have got to acknowledge if you're going to move forward with your wife and daughter."

"Can we stop for today?"

"No. Not just yet. I want a commitment out of you. You told me you were having a luncheon date with your family and Smith."

"Yes."

"I want you to cancel it."

"I can't do that."

"What's the big deal? You just call up this…blues artist and tell him it's off."

"You don't do that to Randall Smith."

"And that's why you're never going to move forward with your family. Bill, you have got to make a choice."

"That's putting me on a rack and stretching my being."

"Exactly."

That evening when Bill went home he knew he had no intention of calling off the lunch date with Smith. It would be like the Pope cancelling Easter. It wouldn't be right – plain and simple.

"Dorothy," said Bill as he came through the front door, "My psychologist wants me to cancel our lunch with Randall."

"Are you going to do it?"

"No dice. I wouldn't treat Randall that way."

"You're right you know. You shouldn't treat a man of Randall's stature that way."

"I don't know if my sessions with Ms. Seneca are helping or hurting me."

"What does she tell you?"

"I don't know if you can handle it."

"Try me."

"We get into the 'my words' or 'Randall's words' thing."

"You're right. I can't handle it."

"Dorothy. Dorothy. Sometimes I wonder..."

"Bill it's just too close to home."

"Why it is we should talk about it."

"Why can't we just leave it alone?"

"You're the one that brought the whole issue out into the light."

"And now I'm turning off the lamp."

"Just like that? You're pulling down the shades?"

"Yes. Just like that."

Dorothy had been sitting in a chair. She got up and went into the kitchen. Bill followed her.

"I can't just shut off my heart like a faucet Dorothy."

"What you do with yourself is with yourself. I'm a separate person with my own needs and desires. You have got to learn to control yours."

"My psychologist thinks I don't know my needs and desires."

"That I can believe."

"What a predicament women place me in."

"Now you're blaming women for your problems?"

"How can I win?"

"You seem to think it's some kind of contest."

Dorothy went back into the living room with Bill right after her.

"Dorothy, I am not in a contest with you."

"Then what's this about not winning?"

Bill was stumped on that one.

"Well…what I meant…what I was trying to say…"

"Bill, I really believe that you do not know what you want."

There was no sympathy in her voice, just a bald declaration.

"Do you have to be so cold? My heart feels the ice."

"It's probably the same ice I felt from you for the first 20 years of our marriage."

"How can you say that?"

"We have a daughter that is the by-product of our failure."

"Well now you're talking about something we can change. We don't have to continue to fail her. We can find her and lift her up."

"If it's not too late."

"Kids grow up late these years."

"Bill do you have to make a joke?"

"Who's joking?"

Dorothy sighed. "Why don't we have dinner?"

"Who's cooking?"

Sara sat in the mess hall with the other inmates. Lunch was baloney sandwiches and potato chips. Luckily her lawyer, Gonzalez had brought her money so she could buy something at the commissary later. The women in her jail were mostly women with medical conditions especially mental illness. Sara was only beginning to be able to comprehend her own condition and situation.

The dream of her being the Virgin Mary meant that she thought she was a lot more pure than the others. She was special in God's eyes and had a clear mission, namely to bring her son Jesus Christ back to earth.

Sara was setting up this scenario pretty much 24-7-365. It meant that people had to see the light of Christ so they'd recognize Him when He came. To Sara, Christ had well defined boundaries which she could clearly see. Yet she realized most people did not see the light.

Nonetheless, they saw a variety of the light that she could relate to. For some people, money was the light. This was true for more people than Sara wanted to imagine. People of other faiths also had their light that they followed that was similar to the light that guided Sara.

However, the other people always seemed to veer off in one errant direction or another which made Sara think she had the one and only true answer.

Now, as Sara sat eating her lunch at Rikers she understood that these people were not open to full acceptance of her direction. At best, she could only get a partial following. It was frustrating to her because she felt she had given her all to get people to see her light.

Sara had gone as far as giving her story to the New York Times even when it meant that she was stepping on her father's toes – no, stomping on them. Everything she did was justified by the light or so she thought.

Vague ideas were coming up with her concerning the question of why she was in jail in the first place. If she was so aligned with God, then why had they locked her up? Why didn't God intervene as she wished? This was the point she had come to. Was God ever going to come back? Was she the one who could bring God to earth? Her days had been motivated by this desire yet it had brought her to ruin in all measures of well-being.

Never taught how to handle ideas this big, this urgent, Sara was at a loss. She simply tried to fit in with whatever environment she was placed into. It goes without saying that a young woman raised in a well-to-do household was struggling with her new-found poverty. She only got by by believing in Christ's non-materialistic message that he had preached 2000 years ago. She just thought, this is what religious people do.

Sara was not holding out for any monetary reward that would come her way through her devotion to Jesus. Her reward would just be the justice of seeing Jesus in the world.

Sara saw people as heathens who had no appreciation for the true message of God. This is why she was able to relatively accept her position among prisoners in jail. If all people were sinners she might as well join the biggest sinners amongst them.

Sara, you have no logic to your thoughts. Sara was admonishing herself. *You can't think your way out of a paper bag.* Sara was at a critical point. *You have to button down the hatch. You have to suck it up. Keep a stiff upper lip.*

The other women began looking at Sara. They noticed that she was into her own head, Then, one spoke.

"Hey, Spacehead, how's the air up there?"

This rankled Sara's soul. *I had been having such deep thoughts.*

"I don't know. How's the garbage in your mind?"
"Say what, white woman?"
A correction officer moved over in their direction. That ended any further confrontation.

When Sara got back to the activity room in the jail, a CO told her that she had a visitor.

"Hi Sara."
"Hi, Ms. Gonzalez."
"Good news Sara. Jim is applying for Mental Health Court."
Sara uttered a non-committal "Oh."
"Sara, I thought you'd be happy."
"Oh, I am," said Sara with the enthusiasm of seaweed.
"Sara, what is it?"
"I almost got in a fight at lunch."
"Oh?"
"I just want my own space, my own life."
"What do you mean Sara?"
Gonzalez was really hoping that Sara was giving up her Virgin Mary delusion.
"I don't want to be the Virgin Mary anymore."
"I would encourage you to give that up."
Ms. Gonzalez said it with a degree of levity that Sara found difficult to comprehend as if Sara's struggle was totally inconsequential.

Sara said with a winching face, "I guess I know I should do that."

This was at once a relief and something repulsive. It took a huge burden off Sara's shoulders but was replaced with the deflating idea that she was giving up on God. God had given her the idea, or at least that's how Sara saw it, and to reject it at this point seemed like a total sellout. However, Ms. Gonzalez was not the person Sara chose to reveal these inner thoughts to.

"When do I get out of here?" asked Sara.

"We're hoping to get you and Jim into Court next week." Ms. Gonzalez did notice that Sara seemed to be harboring some inner turmoil but she professionally avoided any direct confrontation. The attorney realized Sara was already dealing with way too much confrontation both with others and a major confrontation with herself.

"It will be none-to-soon," and Sara managed a small smile.

"All right then. They'll be some interviews, assessments, and a whole lot of paperwork to go through before then. I'd like you to get started by filling out some of these releases of information about you to, oh, about a dozen parties."

"What's a release?"

"Just a formality. It means we can share your personal information with some other people."

"I've got to do it?"

"If you want to move forward, Sara. Yes."

Sara didn't really know up from down, but the idea of moving forward sounded good to her, and she signed the papers. Ms. Gonzalez was the type who really did not like the idea of jumping through a bunch of hoops, but she had learned in law school to follow the rules.

"Thanks Sara. I'll probably see you tomorrow."

"Where are you going now?" asked Sara like a child questioning a parent.

"I'm going over to see your friend, Jim."

In a short time, Sara was reading the New York Times. She had become interested in reading it especially since she and her family had been regular gossip in its pages.

15

The day of Sara's and Jim's debut in the Manhattan Mental Health Court came. Sara actually wore a dress and a bit of make-up and Jim wore a dress shirt and tie. Jack Somany, a judge in the state court system, was presiding. Maria Gonzalez and Scott Jensen were there also. Sara's and Jim's social workers were there as well. They were all gathered in the judge's chambers.

"So, Sara and Jim, what do you have to say for yourselves?" asked Judge Somany.

"Sara and I are both very thankful…" started Jim,

But Sara broke in, "I know what we did was wrong, but I don't understand why we had to go to jail."

"That's why you're in Mental Health Court. You can't comprehend the charges against you," said Jensen.

``Do you have to be so blunt?" interjected Gonzalez.

"Whoa. Everybody slow down. Take a deep breath. Let's not forget the decorum of the court of law."

Judge Somany leaned forth in his chair.

"Judge, I'm a little scared," said Jim.

"What's there to be scared about?" asked the judge. "You're amongst friends."

"I just don't want to blow this chance we're getting," replied Jim.

"Relax Jim. We didn't do nothing," said Sara.

"Wait. Wait right there, young lady," said Jensen. "You're in Mental Health Court because you pled guilty to the charges before you. These charges will only be waved when you have fulfilled your obligations to the court."

Sara said, "I only meant we didn't do anything serious."

"Any offense is serious." Jensen wasn't budging.

"If we can just have a little order here," pleaded the judge. "I am just interested in hearing from both of you that you intend to play by the rules. I'm hearing that from Jim but not so much from you Sara," said Somany as he stared directly into the face of Sara.

"Judge, I always play by the rules," said Sara which surprised just about everybody except herself.

"O.K. Sara. I'm going to hold you to that. Now let's proceed to the courtroom."

The judge got up and led the group down the hall to the courtroom.

Once there, they reviewed the plans for both Sara and Jim. The social workers went over what would be expected of them, and the attorneys discussed time frames and logistics. This lasted about a half hour. Then Judge Somany addressed the two defendants.

"Now that the plans have been laid out before you can you both tell me how you are going to carry them out? Jim, you go first."

Jim was sitting.

"Approach the bench," said Somany.

"Yes sir."

Jim slowly walked up to in front of the judge.

"Well judge, I just want to say that I'm very thankful. I know I could have gone to jail. I won't blow this opportunity."

"Son, I appreciate your words, but tell me how you're going to carry out the plans that have been made for you."

"I expect I'll work with my social worker...I'll..."

Just then Sara rose up. "We will both move into my parents' house and be under their guidance."

Normally a judge would not tolerate this kind of interruption much less respond to it in any positive manner, but the judge turned his attention to Sara.

"Young lady, approach the bench."

The judge folded his powerful hands in front of him and cocked his head sideways.

"Where do these words come from young lady?"
"I think it'll be a good thing." Sara stood unflappable.
"There has been no mention of this in the plan."
"You had us going back to the Washington Lodge, but I think it would be better to go back home."
"Home is always a good place. However, it's not always a possibility. Have you discussed this with anyone?"
"No. It just now popped into my head."
"Everything else aside, don't you think we'd need your parents' approval on such a matter?"
"I was hoping it could be court ordered."
At this point Jim stood up.
"Judge Somany, I'm not sure the things Sara is saying make sense."
This caused a deep hush. Then Gonzalez spoke.
"Jim, you may not know this but the whole reason you're in Mental Health Court and not jail is because Sara demanded it."
Scott Jensen immediately jumped on that.

"Nobody demands nothing of a Court of Law. Everyone is under its precepts."

"Order. Order in the court," demanded Somany.

Everybody returned to their seats.

"Now. A new strategy has been proposed which takes us in a new turn. I realize that Mental Health Court operates a little differently from normal, I mean traditional courts, but it is still a court of law. Certain rules must prevail. I'll have to study the matter this afternoon."

Somany scanned the group.

"Court will recess until tomorrow to consider this alternative plan."

Gonzalez was on her cell to Judge McCutcheon within one minute.

"Bill, we've got to talk. This is Gonzalez."

"Yes. Maria, what can I do for you?"

"Sara dropped a bomb in Mental Health Court today."

"What? What'd she say?"

"She wants the court to place her and her friend, Jim, in your home under your care."

"Oh, this is most unusual and also most opportune."

"How's that Bill?"

"Well Dorothy, my wife, has moved back and we have discussed the very topic."

"So, you'd be O.K. with this?"

"Well, it's certainly a twist to include her friend into our home. Nonetheless, I feel quite strongly that Sara would benefit under Dorothy's and my guidance at this point in her life."

"I'd say we go for it."

When court reconvened the next day, Somany asked Gonzalez to approach the bench.

"Í understand you have been in communication with Judge McCutcheon about the possibility of Sara and Jim moving into his home with his wife Dorothy."

Gonzalez glanced over at Sara and Jim who had already been briefed by her.

"Yes, Judge Somany. Judge McCutcheon is happy to accept Sara back into his home, and Jim too."

"Well, this is an unusual situation. But then again, Mental Health Court is supposed to handle unusual circumstances. I've consulted with the prosecutor and with the social workers, and we feel it could work."

Sara burst forth, "That's great."

"Not so fast Miss McCutcheon. We haven't set the ground rules yet."

Judge Somany asked Sara and Jim to approach the bench.

"The team has come up with five rules that must be followed. If not, your privileges will be rescinded and you'll be channeled back into the criminal justice system. Am I understood?"

"Yes, Judge," said Sara and Jim simultaneously.

"Rule 1. You will stay in the home and only leave when you've been granted permission by Judge McCutcheon and/or his wife.

"Rule 2. Your money will be held by the Judge and Dorothy. They are your payees."

"Rule 3. You must attend 25 meetings for chemical dependency a month for the first six months. You also must show progress in your mental health recovery as measured by your guardians."

"Rule 4. In general, you must submit to all demands of the Judge and Dorothy.

"Rule 5. After one year you must make plans to find a home and occupation outside of the Judge's home."

Judge Somany stared down at the pair of defendants.

"Are we in agreement?"

"Yes, your honor," said Jim. "O.K.," said Sara.

"Now, Ms. Gonzalez, would you go out into the hall and tell Judge McCutcheon and his wife that Sara and Jim are ready to be received into their care?"

Sara and Jim were hardly prepared to move into the McCutcheon home. How could they be? They had coexisted at the Lodge, been pals on the streets, and in jail at the same time, but they were not ready to fall into a routine under Bill and Dorothy. This is unless everyone was ready for change.

"Hi Bill. Hi Mom," said Sara in the hallway of the court building.
"Hi Judge McCutcheon. Hi Mrs. McCutcheon."

Jim felt like the odd man out.

"Oh Jim, just call us Mom and Dad," said Dorothy as Bill stood erect trying to smile.
"Well now. I suppose you're hungry. I fix you lunch when we get back to the Tudor."
Dorothy looked at Bill like what's next?
"We took the train in so we'll take the train home. I do it every day. Well today I didn't because I wasn't judge. Wait, I did take the train in…with Dorothy."
Jim and Sara looked at them like teenagers trying to figure out how square their parents really were.

The train ride was mostly uneventful. They came in the door in White Plains just as the clock was donging the noon hour.

"I'll grab lunch," said Dorothy. She walked into the kitchen.
"Now where do you two have your things?" asked Bill.
"That's a good question, Bill. I'm hoping my stuff is still where I left it under the road."
"What?" asked Bill.
"There was a little nook where I slept. Just below the road. In Manhattan."
"Would you be able to find it again?" asked Bill.
"Of course."
"We'll go there tomorrow. One more day won't make a difference." Bill looked over at Jim. "How about you?"

"My stuff is at the Lodge. That is if they haven't thrown it out." Jim looked a little sheepish.

"Call over there, Jim. Here, use our phone."

Bill directed him to a landline, yes landline phone.

Millie told Jim they had been thinking about getting rid of his stuff but hadn't yet.

"So tomorrow our plan will be to go to Manhattan to get Sara's stuff, then Long Island to get Jim's stuff."

They had lunch.

"Now Jim and Sara, let me show you to your rooms." Bill started up the staircase.

"I've got my old room don't I, Bill?" asked Sara.

"Yes. That is my plan," said the judge.

"And you, Jim, will have the guest room."

Bill showed Jim his room while Sara checked out hers. Jim's room had a window that looked out to the West. There was a double bed and an oak dresser. On the floor was a Persian rug, and a lamp was on the dresser. A print by Monet was on one of the walls.

"Wow, this is great Judge, I mean Dad," said Jim. "I really dig Monet."

"That's fine," said Bill. "Why don't you get situated, take a nap if you'd like. Here. Here's the New Yorker. Read that."

"Wow, that's great, Dad. I really dig the New Yorker."

"Yes. Yes, that fine," said Bill.

Then he walked out of the room leaving Jim in his new home.

Within, five minutes there was a knock on the door.

"Let me in." It was Sara.

Jim opened the door a crack. "I'm not sure we're supposed to talk to each other right now."

"Don't go sappy on me Jim. I just wanted to know if everything is O.K."

"Yes. Why wouldn't it be?"

"Just checking. I'm used to Bill and Dorothy, but I didn't know how you'd take to them."

"Too soon to tell," said Jim.

16

The day after the move-in, Bill, Sara, and Jim got in the Jaguar and headed into Manhattan. Once there Sara directed Bill to the place where she had slept when she was homeless. They parked the car and walked to the spot. Sara walked up the hill and found her stuff still there. As she was coming down, Bill and Jim were talking.

"That's the place Sara was raped," said Jim.
"What?" said Bill and Sara simultaneously.
"I didn't..." began Bill.
"Jim, I hadn't told anyone but you."

Sara was despondent.

"Sara, I'm sorry," said Jim. "I figured your dad knew."

"Sara? You were raped honey?"

Bill was shocked.

"No big deal."

"Didn't you report it to the police?" asked Bill.

"What are they going to do? They'd never believe a homeless girl."

Sara turned away and kicked the air.

"Oh Sara. I am so sorry."

Tears were welling in the eyes of Bill.

"I got over it," said Sara.

"Honey?"

Bill was still in disbelief.

"Happens all the time."

"This time it happened to you," said Jim.

"Let's go. Let's go get Jim's stuff in Long Island."

Sara began walking back to the car and the other two followed.

They got to the car and got in.

Bill was of the opinion that it was not good to try to start a free and open discussion with the three of them. On some level, he thought mental illness belonged in the closet. He was the judge in the Mental Health Court yet he believed that with his own daughter it was best not to engage her in conversation about her illness. He couldn't bear the pain of seeing her this way, nor could he fathom the depth of her affliction and needs.

"It's a pretty nice day isn't it," said Bill as he drove towards Long Island.

"If you like cloudy cold ones," said Sara of the gray September day.

"Oh, look at that man. He's in short sleeves and shorts," observed Bill.

"Let's not talk about people," said Sara.

"I was just making an innocent comment."

"Keep your thoughts to yourself."

"Hey that's a cool building." Jim jumped in.

"It's O.K. to talk about buildings."

Then there was silence until they reached the Washington Lodge. When they got out of the car, Millie came out on the front steps.

"So, let me get this straight," said Millie. "Jim is living at Judge McCutcheon's house with Sara as a part of therapy."

Sara broke in at that and said, "It's not therapy."

"Then what is it exactly Sara?"

"It's a recovery model. Just like Fairweather Lodges. Like what you live in, Millie."

"Mr. McCutcheon, I wish you a lot of luck."

Millie had not let up one hair on her aversion to Sara.

"We won't be needing luck as much as understanding," said the judge.

"Oh, I understand Sara."

"Can I just get my stuff," said Jim.

"I ain't stopping you," said Millie. "Help yourself."

"Millie there's at least one thing I don't miss about living here," said Sara.

"And what's that?"

"You."

That night at the McCutcheon home, the four residents were gathered at the dining room table and were eating dinner. Dorothy had prepared spaghetti which was Sara's favorite.

"So tonight, we're all in for the evening," said Dorothy. "Tomorrow Bill's gotta work, and I'll have some stuff around the house for you two kids."

"I'm not really a kid, Dorothy," said Sara.

"As long as you're living at my house rent free you'll not call me Dorothy and you will be a kid."

"Wait a min…"

"I will not hear you talk back to me, Sara."

Sara knew her alternative to living at home was jail, and she wasn't going to go there again.

"Yes, Mom. I'll do what I'm asked…but no more."

"You'll do what you're asked and you'll like it," said Dorothy.

Sara knew Dorothy was not the soft touch that her father was.

"Right," was all she said.

Then Bill spoke. "So, Sara and Jim, why don't you go on line this evening and find out about some AA groups. You'll have to get going quick to get 25 meetings in this month."

"Hold on Bill," said Dorothy. "I had a few projects I wanted them to tackle."

Bill looked at his watch. "It's only six o'clock. There's time to do both."

"I'll get the painting equipment ready while they look for 12 step groups."

"Painting equipment?" Sara said insolently.

"Sara, you'll do as you're told."

Dorothy placed both hands on the table in front of her.

"I will have you and Jim paint the rooms where you're staying."

Jim, who had been silent, said, "That sounds like a great idea, Mom."

They talked about colors and possible transportation to meetings during the rest of dinner.

"Dad, can we use the computer in your office to go on-line?" asked Jim as they were finishing the meal.

"Sure," said Bill. "Feel free."

Jim and Sara got up from the table, walked through the living room, and to a solid wood door which opened to Bill's office.

Sara booted up the PC.

"Bill uses Google," said Sara.

She typed in *AA White Plains NY*

"Oh wow," said Sara. "They've got AA groups every day of the week at Memorial Methodist. That's Bill's and Mom's church."

"You're kidding."

"No, look."

"Let's check it out tomorrow."

Jim looked into Sara's eyes.

"Yeah. We'll have to work it around Mom's plans."

"Do you think she'll give us the car," asked Jim.

"I don't see why not. My license has been renewed."

"Sara, we have a plan."

Dorothy knocked on the door.

"Yes?" said Sara.

"I've got a couple of scrapers," said Dorothy. "You two ready?"

"We don't have to scrape do we?" moaned Sara.

"We've already painted over once. This time we scrape," said Dorothy.

In a short time, Jim and Sara, each in their own room, were scraping the paint off the plaster walls. Jim was scraping blue paint, and Sara was scraping yellow.

Dorothy came into Jim's room.

"I'm planning on buying the paint tomorrow," said Dorothy. "Do you have any color preferences?"

Jim said, "Just what I said at dinner. Light blue is fine."

Dorothy went to Sara's room.

"Sara?"

"Yes, Mom."

"What color do you want to paint your room?"

"Pink."

"What?!"

"You act surprised."

"Well...it's just that...well...that's a girl's color."

"In case you haven't noticed, I am a girl."

"It's been a long time that you, well, I'll be blunt, you haven't been very ladylike."

"That's all changing."

"Sara, am I hearing you right?"

"You and Dad want me to be a woman, don't you?"

"Well...yes."

"So, I'm not stupid. I either sink or I swim. You and Dad are helping me and I need all the help I can get."

"But when did you start thinking this way?"

"It kind of started when I got rid of Bain. It's been a long time coming. Having Jim as a friend just solidifies it."

"Sara, I'm very, very, very pleased. Pink it shall be."

Dorothy turned around and left as Sara nonchalantly

continued scraping.

A couple hours later Bill made the rounds.

"Time to knock it off and go to bed," he told Jim and Sara, and they both got ready and went to bed.

In the morning at 6:00 o'clock, Bill got everybody up.

"So, I'd like us to start our day with a short meditation," said Bill.

"Meditation?" exclaimed Sara.

"Just something I wrote," said Bill.

"I think that's great, Mr. McCut...I mean Dad," said Jim.

"Let's hear it," said Dorothy.

Bill began, "A man went out walking. He was going to the grocery store. He came to a corner. There were two ways he could go. Both would take him there. One way was short and easy. Simple. The other way was long and winding. There were hills and detours. At times the road was quite narrow. Other times it was quite broad.

"The man paused only a minute before he chose the harder road. He knew his experience would be richer going that way. It would be more challenging but potentially more rewarding.

"It took him two hours to get to the store, but when the grocer asked him how his day was going, he didn't have to lie when he said, 'It's been a trip.'"

Then Bill looked at the three listeners and said, "Make the right choice about the path you choose today."

It wasn't two seconds when Sara said, "Dad I was going to ask to use the car to go to my 12-step meeting. Instead I am going to dig out my bike, and can Jim use yours?"

Dorothy said, "I'm going to walk to the paint store."

All Bill could say was, "Well, well."

When Bill arrived at the courthouse, he noticed he was short of breath even though he had hardly exerted himself. He quickly dismissed the observation and said hi to Molly who faithfully greeted him like he was her hero and not a judge who had been in his role in the Mental Health Court for just one year.

"Hi, Bill."

"Hi, Molly."

"There are a couple new candidates for Mental Health Court. Their files are on your desk."

"Thanks, Molly. Anything else?"

"Well there was a call from a certain musician, but nobody you'd…yes, Randall Smith called!"

"You serious?"

"As a mirror."

"I don't know how serious a mirror is, but…"

"Mirrors are very serious Bill, and yes, he did call. Said he'd call back."

"I'll be in my chambers."

Bill was in his office and looking at the new files when Smith called.

"Randall, what can I do for you?"

"Just calling about our get together. Do you have a place and time yet?"

"Yes. The *New Yorker*. October 6, at 2 P.M."

"Great. I've been there before. Just want to run something by you."

"Go ahead, Randall."

"I'm going to have a crew with. I'd like to videotape our outing."

"What?"

"Don't get excited, Judge. I just want to show people that I can be a real guy. You know having lunch with his lawyer and family. You are bringing family right, Judge?"

"Whatever you want Randall. It's yours for the asking."

"Then I'll see you next month at the *New Yorker.* Wear something casual but smart. A judge has to look smart."

"O.K. Randall. O.K."

Bill got up from his desk and walked into Molly's reception office.

"Molly, Randall's going to videotape our lunch date with my family."

"What?"

"He's trying to prove he's just a normal guy."

"Most people try to prove they're something greater than they are. Here's Randall trying to dumb himself down."

"That's the magnitude of the man Molly."

17

Sara was at home one night in the bathroom and looking in the mirror. She was trying to determine whether she liked what she saw. *I'm a little on the chubby side*, she thought. *My cheeks puff out. Luckily, I'm not vain.* She took a deeper look. Into her eyes. *Am I really schizophrenic like the doctors say or am I the Virgin Mary for real? No, I gave that up. Does that leave me with schizophrenia? I am a client in the Mental Health Court. Maybe the meds are controlling the illness. I don't feel sick…but I did. I have been crazy. But that old woman by the school yard. Was she really an angel? Why did she appear to just me? I may not be the Virgin Mary as I thought, but the angel was so good. She gave me light like no one else could. Everyone else says the old woman was a delusion. But how do they know? They don't. They're guessing. I need somebody. Somebody now that can give me light.*

Just then there was a knock on the door.

"Sara?" It was Jim. "How long are you going to be?"
"Can't you use the bathroom downstairs?"
"What?"
Wait a minute thought Sara. *What about Jim? Can he bring light into my life?*
"Jim I'll be right out."
When Sara opened the door, she gave Jim a probing look.
"What's up Sara?"
"Nothing. Just thought for a moment…no nothing."
"Yeah O.K. Sara."
The two went to bed that evening with Sara obsessing on Jim and Jim blissfully unaware.

In the morning Bill had everyone up at the usual 6:00 o'clock.

"I've got another meditation," said Bill.

"A young woman was distraught. She felt she was at the crossroads in life, or maybe even a dead end. She wasn't sure how she was going to be able to go on."

"Wait a minute," interrupted Sara. "Is this about me?"

"Doesn't have to be," said Bill. "Please let me continue."

"Out of seemingly nowhere, an angel appeared."

"This is about me. I know it." Sara was getting edgy.

"Sara, just listen to the story. Read into it what you want."

"Now. An angel appeared and the young woman felt her life go past her. She knew she had to be deathly quiet in order to continue to be able to "see" the angel. There was no great voice, no forceful entry into her heart, just a brightness and a holy sense of God. The woman was in awe. Then she felt her focus slipping. It was heart wrenching to be so close to something like heaven and then feel it slip through her fingers. She knew to her dying day that she must search out the angel in any and every way she could. Her direction in life was set."

Bill looked at the three – Dorothy, Jim, and Sara. "What'd you think?"

Sara quickly said, "It sounds a lot like me, but every time I bring up the topic of me as the Virgin Mary everyone says I'm nuts."

"Sara, it's not as simple as that. When you witness God, you don't become someone else."

"Then what's the point of the angel coming into your life?"

Bill was momentarily knocked off balance by that one, but he regained his sense of control and said, "An angel comes into your life for many reasons. In my story, it was there to reveal God."

"Oh yeah?" said Sara.

"I think at your AA meeting, you have something to talk about Sara."

"I'll let it go at that," Sara replied.

In her past Sara would have never cut off the argument, but things were changing.

Dorothy asked, "How about breakfast? Then I'll drive you to your meeting."

Jim jumped in, "That would be great Mom."

Sara and Jim had been attending meetings for a couple weeks, and they were getting to know some of the people. More importantly they were getting a chance to say their spiel. This was especially important for Sara because she had so many issues in her life that were troubling and confusing.

"Hi, my name is Sara, and I'm an alcoholic."

Everyone said, "Hi Sara."

"I'm still working on the first step. I'm feeling totally powerless over alcohol…and a lot of other things too. I especially feel powerless over other people. My parents for example. I'm feeling the bite of the law too. I just want to be free. Free to do what I want to do. Yet I know that's selfish. I really don't know what I want. I'm 23 years old but I have the emotions of a teenager. All I know is that I got into trouble. Big trouble. I guess I need help. I need a lot of help. That's it."

Everyone said, "Thanks for sharing." And they went around the group until they got to Jim.

"My name is Jim, and I don't know what I am."

A man said, "That's O.K. The only requirement for membership is a desire to stop drinking."

"Yeah I don't want to drink my problems away. I just get depressed when I drink. At first it was fun. As a kid, I mean. My friends…we had a gas. But then it stopped being fun. I got really sad all the time. I didn't want to do anything. I guess I kind of tried to kill myself. That's about the time I met Sara. She knows this stuff about me."

Sara slumped in her chair. She thought, *Jim's saying these things like he's counting on me, but I'm not totally here. I need him to help me, but he's trying to get me to help him. This is heavy stuff. I don't know if I can handle it. Wait. You've made your decision. You know the phrase, "Fake it until you make it."*

A woman next to Sara was starting to look over at her.

Then she whispered, "Are you O.K.?"
Sara whispered back, "I'm fine."
What else could Sara say? *Fake it 'til you make it.*

The meeting lasted an hour.
"Jim, we don't have a way home."

Sara and Jim were standing outside of the church. They had gotten a ride there by Dorothy.

"Let's walk."
"It's about **five** miles," said Jim kind of hesitating and emphasizing the five.
"Jim, you're a man, aren't you?"
"You better believe I am."
"Then let's go."
It was a cool mid-September day. Leaves on the trees were beginning to turn color. Children were playing in the schoolyard. White Plains was slowed down and not much was going on.

"Did you like the meeting?" asked Jim.
"It was like all the others," said Sara.
"It's kind of cool to see people into sobriety, isn't it?"
"I don't know how cool it is,"
"Sara, what's wrong?"
"When I was with Bain…"
"Oh, Sara don't mention him."

"Let me finish if you will. When I was with Bain, he was cool. He was so so cool. I don't want cool anymore. You get so cool you're cold. Nothing matters. You just have to protect an image. You won't let anyone into your life. Nothing is good enough. Everything is beneath you."

"Do you really think so? I've always thought about cool as the calm in the storm. Nothing rattles you. Even keel and all that."

"Cool is an ego trip. It's shallow. Nobody is really cool. They're just good fakers."

"Oh, some people are cooler than others."

"Why do you say that?"

"I think you're cooler than most."

"What? Really? Bain tried to make me out to be a sap."

"You a sap? No. I think you're cool."

"Just the same. Bill and Dorothy always taught me I was beautiful."

"Of course, you are."

"Plus intelligent."

"Yes."

In a little while they were home.

Things marched on for another week without much variance in the tempo of life of the small family or the questions before them.

Then it was time for Sara and Jim to check into Mental Health Court.

Judge Somany presided at the bench.

"Sara and Jim, will you come forward?"

Maria Gonzalez and Scott Jensen remained seated.

"So. I've gotten good reports from all parties concerning your behavior."

"Thank you, judge."

"You've attended your 12 step meetings, yes?"

"Every day."

"Your parents report that you've been obedient. Is this true?"

"Yes judge."

"What's on the horizon for the coming month?"

"We're having lunch with Randall Smith," said Sar0a.

Judge Somany, not knowledgeable about Bill McCutcheon's

connection with Smith, thought that the statement was delusional.

"Oh? Thee Randall Smith?"

"Yes. The blues artist."

Somany cast a forlorn glance over at the two attorneys.

"Have you been taking your medications, Sara?" asked the

judge.

"Yes. Of course."

"Well how did you become under the impression you would be having lunch with Randall Smith?"

"He called my dad."

"Oh. He called your dad."

"Randall Smith and my dad go way back."

"Sara, are you seeing anybody?"

"Just the people in the room here."

"What I mean is, are you seeing anybody who prescribes your meds?"

"Yes."

"Who is that person?"

"Clara Seneca. She's a doctor/psychologist."

"I recommend that you see her soon."

"Sure. Is that it?"

"Isn't that enough?"

Somany looked around the room. A lot of empty looks.

When they got out in the lobby, Gonzalez said to Sara, "Is that one of your delusions Sara?"

"What's that?"

"That your dad knows Randall Smith?"

At that Jensen jumped in. "Oh my god. Maria that's no delusion…Bill does know… oh my god…did Judge Somany think it was a delusion? I should have said something. No…Bill and Randall Smith are friends…and if Sara thinks they're going to have lunch…they probably are."

Gonzalez looked like a football player who had just taken a

blow to the head.

"Then Sara is not delusional."

"I've been trying to tell you that for five years." Sara had a look of eureka.

"No, Sara. Your Virgin Mary thing is delusional. Your Randall Smith thing is not."

Gonzalez spoke with the psycho-medical authority of a psychiatrist.

"Oh, I'm only half-nuts," joked Sara.

"Don't joke about such things Sara," said Jensen. "You're still in hot water."

"They say if you can't stand the heat then get out of the kitchen."

Sara looked combative.

"Let's call it a day," said Gonzalez

18

Bill took the elevator up to the 3rd floor in route to see Clara Seneca.

They exchanged formalities in her office and then Ms. Seneca opened with a question.

"So, you've cancelled your luncheon date with Randall Smith I'm assuming?"

"No, why should I?"

"If Sara is ever going to get to know you, you're going to be required to disassociate yourself from him."

"I will when he dies."

"This is not a joke Mr. McCutcheon and mental illness is no laughing matter."

"Randall Smith is too big a part of my life to forget about him."

"If I am going to work with you you'll have to get rid of him."

"I can't."

"Do you expect me to deal with that?"

"Ms. Seneca, I'm paying you good money to help me resolve my whole life, not just a portion of it."

"Okay, okay. As long as you pay the bills I'll listen. I don't think it's a good way to go, but, hey, money talks."

"That's the first thing we got to get straight. With Randall, it's not about money."

Ms. Seneca burst out laughing.

"You don't think money is important to him? How many times over is he a millionaire?"

"It's his art. He's been quite fortunate to do well financially, but that doesn't take away his way with words."

"About his words. What percentage of your words come out of Smith?"

"Percentage of my words? You make it sound so calculating."

"Let me remind you that we're on the clock."

"I can't believe I'm even seeing you. These accusations, these pronouncements…"

"When Randall Smith dies what are you going to do?"

"I might die before him."

"You seem quite evasive on the subject. Why is that?"

"It's probably my pride."

"A lot of spiritual people think pride is a sin."

"What are you driving at?"

"I just think there are a lot of other worthy spiritual people out there who you seem to pass over."

"For instance?"

"Why don't we start with your daughter, Sara."

"You think I pass over her? I somehow deny her existence?"

"This thing about the Virgin Mary. What's your take on that?"

"I don't know what to say."

"Your daughter thinks she's Mother Mary but you have no opinion on it."

"The mental health system calls her delusional. You are part of the mental health system, aren't you?"

"I see it as a complex issue."

"And how do I see it?"

"You kind of treat her like she's an object."

"An object? Really. I love my daughter."

"Do you love her, or do you love an image of her?"

"I treat things as things and people as people. I use things, not people."

"You think so?"

"I think we have to stop for today."

"We don't have to. But we can if you wish."

"Yes. That's what I wish."

Bill arose almost indignantly out of his chair.

"I'll let you know when I want to see you again, Ms. Seneca."

Sara and Jim were at an AA meeting.

"So, there I was playing soccer, and an elderly lady walked by the field. She smiled at me. Not at any of the others, just at me. I turned to look at the reactions from the others, and when I looked back to see the lady, she was gone. I interpreted it as though she was telling me I was special. Really special. I surmised that she was an angel, and I was the Virgin Mary."

A woman from the group interrupted.

"I don't usually cross-talk in group but this is no ordinary claim. Sara? You think you're the Virgin Mary?"

Sara immediately closed down.

"I'm not talking. I pass to the next person."

The woman continued, "You can't just claim you're the Virgin Mary and then pass."

Sara replied, "The only requirement for membership in AA is a desire to stop drinking. I can say anything I want."

"Okay. All right. Then let's go on."

Jim had been squirming in his chair. After the woman spoke he said, "Yes. Let's go on."

After the meeting concluded, and Jim and Sara were outside the church, Jim tried to broach the topic of Sara's statements about the Virgin Mary. Sara, however, would have none of it. She just walked towards home and Jim followed.

In a cheap apartment in the Bronx Bain Bottles was making a plan.

Let's see. I've got my pistol. I've got duct tape. I've got my duffel bag. I've got my key that Sara gave me a long time ago. I've got my map to Mexico. Should be all I'll need. Tonight's the night.

Bain had his plan. He would take a late-night train into White Plains. At about midnight he would make his move. Everyone at the McCutcheon household would be in bed. Using the key that Sara had once given him, he would go into the home. At gunpoint, he would bind everyone with duct tape except Sara. For her, it would be a choice. Either leave with him willingly, or else under the threat of the gun. He would get car keys and money. Bill, in an out-of-date tradition, had a wall safe. Sara had told Bain about it. Within 15 minutes they would be on their way to Mexico.

Sara may put up a fight at first, but she'll come around. I know she'll choose me over the square way her life is going now.

It was mid-afternoon, Friday, September 21, 2012. Bain laid down on his bed to get rest for the night ahead.

The McCutcheon family sat at dinner.
"What have you kids planned for your evening?" asked Dorothy.
Jim winced but remembered that Dorothy insisted on calling them "kids".
"Oh, we'll probably just play computer games or text the other kids from our support group," said Sara.
"I have a better idea," said Dorothy. "You can clean out the garage."
"That's something you do in the Spring, not the Fall," said Sara.
"It's something you do when it's necessary, and when you have the time."

"Dad? What do you think?" asked Sara knowing her dad to be a softer touch.

"I think you can do both," said Bill diplomatically.

"Computer games first?" asked Sara.

"Yeah, yeah. O.K." said Bill.

Jim and Sara rushed off to the office room.

"Bill, I'll be damned if I know why you're so easy on them."

"Honey I've learned over the years that you have to work with others, not just shove orders at them."

"If you'd have been in the military you'd be singing a different song."

"Honey you know I was against the Viet Nam War."

"Just the same. It might have made a man out of you."

"I'm not a man?"

"Sometimes I wonder."

Bill and Dorothy finished their meal in silence.

When they got up, Dorothy headed to the office room.

"O.K. kids, it's time to clean the garage."

"But it's only been a half hour," said Sara.

"It's going to take you the rest of the night to do the garage," said Dorothy.

Bain got on the Metro North Train at Bronxville Station at 12:19 AM headed to White Plains. He looked a little out of place because he was wearing sunglasses. He arrived at White Plains at 12:33 AM.

He opened his duffel bag and took out a beer which he opened and drank with zest. Then he took out another and another. He didn't stop until he had drunk six beers. He looked around. No one was watching him.

Then he began to put his plan in action. He arrived at the McCutcheon home about 1:30. He fumbled for the key. The key he had was for the garage. Sara had given it to him the night they stole Bill's car. He opened the door and walked in. He didn't get far before there was a loud crash and he was on the ground. What had happened was that Sara and Jim had not finished cleaning the garage and had left a lot of stuff all over which Bain had not seen in the dark.

The noise was loud enough to awaken Jim who was a light sleeper. Jim was just bold enough to go investigate what happened. When he went through the door from the house to the garage he turned on the light and saw Bain. Jim had never seen Bain, and to Jim this man was an unknown intruder.

"What the hell are you doing?" asked Jim.

Bain didn't answer but when he looked down at his bag Jim got nervous and rushed Bain tackling him on the cement floor temporarily knocking him out. Then Jim wrapped his arms around Bain's neck and got him in a full nelson. By this time Bill, Sara, and Dorothy showed up.

"Get the bag," yelled Jim. "See what's in it."

Sara, although in near shock to see Bain this night, quickly grabbed the duffel bag and opened it. She found the gun. By this time Bain had come to and was struggling to free himself from Jim.

"Mutherfucker, I'll kill you," screamed Bain.

"I wouldn't if I were you," said Sara. She pointed the gun at Bain. "Dad, call the police."

Jim could no longer hold Bain down, and Bain broke free.

Bain began slowly approaching Sara.

"Give me the gun, Sara."

"Back the fuck off Bain or I will shoot."

Bain had never seen Sara like this. It took him back.

"Jim, get the tape out of the bag and secure his hands," said Sara. "And his feet."

In a couple of moments Bain was on the floor and going nowhere.

"Sons of bitches, I'll kill you all," shouted Bain.

"Shut the fuck up Bain," screamed back Sara.

"Sara, don't engage him," said Bill.

Dorothy was on the phone calling 911.

Jim was still hyped up and was keeping a nervous eye on Bain.

"What the fuck do you think you were doing, Bain?" Sara couldn't hold back.

"Sara, the police will be here shortly. Try not to talk to him."

Bill, the only one calm in the garage, stood his ground.

"I came to kill you all," shrieked Bain.

"You're a fuckin' flunky Bain," said Sara.

"Sara..." Bill started.

"You can kiss your ass goodbye, Bain." Sara couldn't stop.

"I may do time, but when I get out..." started Bain.

"You'll what, Bain?" asked Sara.

Jim was getting more and more nervous. He hadn't seen this side of Sara. He might have guessed about it, but he had never actually witnessed something like this before.

The police were there within five minutes.

"What's going on here?" asked the officer as he came into the garage.

"We caught him breaking and entering..."

"I had a key," shouted Bain.

The officer looked at Bain. Sara was still holding the gun.

"That his gun?" asked the cop.

"Yes, sir," said Sara.

"Do you know the guy?" asked the policeman.

"Unfortunately," said Sara. "He came into our house and my boyfriend Jim subdued him."

"Boyfriend? That wimp?'" said Bain.

"He took care of you, didn't he Bain?"

Sara was still highly agitated.

The officer looked at Bill. "This your house?"

"Yes."

The officer leaned over Bain and put cuffs over the tape. Then he pulled Bain up off the floor.

"I'm taking him in. I'll be in touch."

The policeman walked Bain to the squad and put him in. He talked with Bill for a few minutes.

"Officer, this is his duffel bag and gun," said Dorothy walking over the car. "You might want it for evidence."

"I suggest you try to get a good night of sleep," said the cop as he got into his car.

Then he drove off.

19

The next morning Bill hadn't been in the office five minutes when he got a call from Scott Jensen, the prosecutor.

"Little fireworks out at your house last night, Bill?" asked Jensen.

"Don't tell me you know already," said Bill.

"Word like that travels fast. Say, this might be another one for Mental Health Court."

"Oh, no. Not this time. No, Scott, no."

"Little change in stance, Bill? You always said give guys the benefit of a doubt."

"Scott, he had a gun."

"Turns out it wasn't loaded. Says he forgot to load it."

"Doesn't make a difference in the eyes of the law."

"The kid told me he never pointed it. He said it was in his bag until the other guy grabbed it."

"He broke into our house."

"He said he had a key given to him by your daughter."

"What are you charging him with?"

"Creating a disturbance."

"You have lost it Scott."

"Kind of different when you're on the other side of the coin, heh?"

"Scott, give me a call when you've come to your senses. Goodbye."

"Molly, could you come into my chambers, please?"

Molly knocked on the door and entered.

"Bill? What is it?"

`"You remember that boy who I thought was bad company for Sara?"

"Yes, I remember something about him. What about him?"

"He broke into our house last night. I don't know his exact plans, but they weren't good."

"Seriously."

"Now Scott wants to place him in Mental Health Court."

"Really."

"Seems there is nothing more that Scott likes than to upset me."

"Wonder why that is?"

"Some twisted sense of competition."

"You guys, I don't know sometimes."

"Don't include me in on that, Molly. I try to always be fair."

"Yes of course you do."

"What is it, Molly? Are you O.K.?"

"What do you mean, Bill?"

"You just don't seem all there. You have so little reaction to what I'm telling you."

"Your senses are very acute, Bill." Molly sat down. "There is something. It's just that now didn't seem to be a good time, but I suppose there never will be a good time…"

"Say it, Molly."

"Bill, I plan to retire."

"Oh. Wow." Bill leaned back in his chair. "When?"

"I can give you two months, Bill."

"Molly, have you thought it over? Is there something I did?"

"Yes. I've thought it over, and no, it's not you. It's just time, Bill."

"Well O.K. You'll go with my best wishes."

"Thanks, Bill. I knew I could count on you."

"Just promise to come in from time to time and see me."

Sara arrived at Ms. Seneca's building.

"Hi, Ms. Seneca," said Sara as she came into the office.

Ms. Seneca asked, "How have you been, Sara?"

"Same old same old."

"Nothing new? No developments?"

"Well my old boyfriend tried to break into our house the other night."

"WHAT? Wait a minute. Go back."

"We caught Bain in our garage. He had a gun."

"That doesn't sound good, Sara."

"No, I suppose it isn't."

"Aren't you a little shocked…scared?"

"I think the whole thing is a bit ludicrous. I have no idea of what he was up to."

"People don't just break into someone's house. Couldn't you see it coming?"

"I had cut him off…out of my life. I suppose it was some kind of revenge thing. The scary thing is he had a gun."

"Dear child. You have been through so much."

"It seems non-ending. I don't know how much more I can take."

"Don't give up hope. You always have hope."

Sara looked around the room and up at the ceiling.

"I guess I still have my angel."

"Angel?"

"The one who revealed to me that I'm the Virgin Mary."

"Don't go there, Sara."

"Why not?"

"It's not good for you." Ms. Seneca looked nervous.

"It's the best hope I have."

154

"It's out of this world, Sara."

"You would rather see me docile. Taking meds and being a little mouse."

"Sara, that's not it."

"Isn't it though?"

"Sara, your mind is sick. You need medication to help you."

"I'm just sick of all the sin I see in the world."

"There always will be sin."

"Not if I bring Jesus back to earth."

"Has he contacted you about this, Sara?"

"No, but the rock stars sing about it in their songs."

"That's their art. It's an expression. Doesn't make it based on fact."

"Yeah, so?"

"You're not an artist. You don't understand."

"I'm an experienced woman."

"Sara, I don't think you're comfortable with your dark side."

"Wait. Just a minute. Dark side?!"

"Everybody's got a dark side, Sara."

"Jesus didn't."

"Do you want to end up like him?"

"There's just so much ugliness in the world. We need more light."

"How are we going to do that, Sara?"

"Bring Jesus back?"

"He might not want to come back. Did you ever think of that?"

"How would you know?"

"I don't think anyone knows."

"I believe the angel was giving me the message to bring him back."

"Maybe the angel was just telling you you're special."

"That's what I'm trying to say."

"But to be the Virgin Mary and usher Christ back to the world? Sounds a little farfetched."

"You underestimate me, Ms. Seneca."

"And I think you underestimate other people."

"I think that's enough for today."

"If you say so."

The next day Bill was in his chambers when he got another call from Scott Jensen, the prosecutor. It wasn't even 7:35 AM yet.

"So, Bill, I'd really like to move forward on this."

"This?"
"Bain Bottles. Mental Health Court. You know."
"Give it up, Scott."
"The boy's got potential. I've seen evidence of remorse."
"I don't…"
"I'm going to bring him in with Maria Gonzalez tomorrow. He's got a Social Worker. We'll have a plan. Everything will be fine."

"Somehow I don't think I have a choice, Scott."

The following morning Jensen, Gonzalez, and Bottles were standing in the hall when the judge got off the elevator.

"Good morning, Bill." Jensen was all smiles.
Bottles was all smiles too. "Good morning Judge."
Gonzalez was the only one of the three who seemed even vaguely aware of Bill's feelings.

"Hi, Judge McCutcheon. Under the circumstances I won't ask how you are doing."
"Good morning, group," said Bill. "Why don't we head to my chambers?"
"Judge, are you going to go easy on me?"
Bain looked in-between serious and mocking.
"What do you think, Bain?"
The judge was as stoic as the marble walls.

When they had all been seated in the judge's chambers Judge McCutcheon began laying down the law.

"First off Bain. This is against my will. If it was my choice you'd do time. But since my esteemed…"
"Esteemed?' interjected Jensen.

"O.K. my colleague Scott Jensen is forcing the issue, it will move forward. But I am not going to be easy on you, Bain because I don't think you deserve it or that your actions that night should be taken lightly. You will leave here today on your own recognizance but you will be wearing an ankle bracelet…"

"Wait a minute, Judge," Gonzalez tried to stop him.

"Ms. Gonzalez, please do not interrupt. Bain, you will be required to check in hourly with your social worker. Anytime you go anywhere you must call and ask for permission. You can only eat healthy food. No pop. No candy. Random checks will be made at your apartment. If any unauthorized food is found you will be out of the program. You must do your laundry in the sink and let it dry in your room. No going downstairs to the laundromat. If you have cable TV cancel it. You will only have 5 CD's in your possession. Of course, it goes without saying, no computers, no internet, and no Ipods or any other electronic devices. So, the five CD's are really useless. That's about it. No wait. You will be required to read 4 hours a day and submit handwritten reports. There. That does it. Are you clear?"

Bain looked like he had just received a death penalty.

"Yes."

"Yes what?"

"Yes, sir."

Everyone in the room was stunned, but the fierceness of the judge's declaration had put the fear of God into them.

"Can I go?" asked Bain

"Your social worker will escort you now," said the judge.

Jensen and Gonzalez remained in the room after Bain left.

"You sure you're not being too soft on him, Bill?" asked Jensen.

"Bottles never belonged here, Scott. Just be thankful I'm working with him."

"Judge McCutcheon, I've never seen you like this." Gonzalez was stunned.

"It happens, Maria. Do you have children?"

"No. No I don't."

"Well when your child has been taken down by a bad force, then you just don't have the patience for that bad force."

"Oh. I see what you mean."

"I hope you do."

The rest of the day Bill stayed in his chambers with the door shut. Mostly he just stared at the wall.

Sara and Jim were asking permission from Dorothy to go to their AA meeting.

"Mom, it's about that time," said Sara.

"Time?" asked Dorothy.

"Jim and I should be going to our AA meeting."

"Are you asking my permission?"

"Judge Somany laid down that rule."

"I just don't know if I can take the responsibility to tell you what you can and can't do."

"Mom, you've been doing it over three weeks. What's different today?"

"I just don't like the way things are going."

"What are you talking about?"

"It's Bill, your father. I think something is going on with him."

Sara looked perplexed. She didn't have a clue.

"Your father is losing his hair. I find it in the drain. And at night he has trouble with his breathing. Shortness of breath."

"Oh yeah?"

"It's like his health is deteriorating."

"Mom, that's not like him. Have you said anything to him?"

"You know we don't talk about things that matter."

"And why is that, Mom? Why is that?"

"It's just our relationship."

"No, Mom. Growing up I thought you and Dad had a fantastic relationship."

"You did?"

"Yeah. Every family has problems, but you and Dad and me...we were great."

"Sara, that's not the way things turned out."

"I know. A lot of it is my fault."

"Sara, don't start that. I can't bear to see you take all the blame."

"Someone's got to take it."

"Then blame your father."

"What?!"

"He was the one who was never there for you."

"I don't see why we have to blame someone."

Sara was taken back.

"Sara, you just said somebody's got to take the blame."

"Well I don't think it should be Dad."

"Who then?"

"Me." Sara thrust out her chest.

Jim was feeling very awkward but remained silent.

"Sara, you've got to learn to pass the buck. You can't shoulder blame for everything, everybody."

"There's too much blame-passing in society. I take full responsibility for bringing Jesus into the world."

"What on earth?"

"I'm the Virgin Mary so I brought Jesus into the world."

"When did you do that, Sara? I never knew about it."

"It's foggy in my memory…"

"Sara, are you still taking your medication?"

"Well…no…I stopped."

"Sara, what am I going to do?" Dorothy was in tears.

"O.K. O.K. Mom. I'll start them again."

"Sara, it's not a game. You don't just take medication when you feel like it."

"I know, Mom. I know."

"I just don't think we should tell your father. He's got enough worries."

Sara hung her head.

"Go up to your bathroom Sara and take a double dose right now."

"I don't think it works like that, Mom. I'll get back on track. Don't worry."

"And get that Virgin Mary thing out of your head. Don't go there."

20

Bill was in session with Ms. Seneca.

"So, what does your doctor say about this shortness of breath, loss of hair?" asked Ms. Seneca.

"Doctor?"

"Yes. Your medical doctor."

"I haven't seen a doctor in a while."

"A while?"

"Couple of years."

"You? A professional man almost 60 years old? Don't go to the doctor?"

"I've been healthy. Saw no need."

"Then why are you telling me about it now?"

"Well I'm worried now…a little."

"I'm not your medical doctor. I don't monitor your physical health."

"I'm really concerned about how this would impact Sara...and also Dorothy."

"You sound like you're dying."

"I just don't feel zip in my system." Bill shrugged.

"How are you doing with this?" Ms. Seneca was concerned.

"I'm O.K. myself but I worry especially for Sara."

"She's quite dependent on you. You're aware of that, aren't you?"

"She's got this friend..."

"That boy that broke into your house?"

"Heavens no...wait. How did you know about that?"

"God. I tried so hard not to bring your two stories together."

"What?"

"You and Sara. I didn't want any cross-talking."

"What's cross-talking?"

"Bringing Sara into your session or you into Sara's session."

"We are family you know."

"I realize this Mr. McCutcheon." Clara looked up and sighed. "I just thought it better to keep you two separate."

"You're a human being. You're fallible."

"It's just a mistake I can't afford to make."

"It'll wash."

"How can you be so blasé?" asked Ms. Seneca.

"I don't see what the big deal is."

"You've got a daughter with a major mental illness. Your health is going down the tubes, but you can't tell your family. And you don't think there's a problem?"

"Well I didn't say there wasn't a problem."

"So how do you expect me to fix it now? I was trying to give each of you a life. A separate life. You know different from each other."

"And because I know Sara talked to you about Bain, that spoils the whole thing?"

"I don't think you comprehend how difficult my job is. You seem to be so naïve."

"I've been told that before, but..."

"You probably don't realize that Sara might have a sexual attraction to you."

"What now?"

"So many things just go right past you."

"I'm in a difficult position."

"How so?"

"Sara either thinks I'm the biggest ass this side of Pluto, or that I walk on water. Dorothy says I'm a stuffed shirt with no ideas of my own."

"What do you think?" Clara leaned forward. "It's most important what you think."

"I'm somewhere in the middle. I mean I can be real tough on Sara, but I think she needs that. I'm trying to help her find herself which is exactly what Dorothy says I haven't done in my own life."

"And…"

"So, I'm thinking Dorothy is giving me a bum rap on the Randall Smith thing. Smith was a star, and I bought the ticket. I didn't feel like living in the murky darkness that most people do. Smith offered me light, and I held up the torch. What's so different from what a lot of Christians say about Jesus?"

"Jesus was God. Smith is not God."

"What's your definition of God?"

"You're getting close to blasphemy now." Clara looked threatened.

"What?! Because I ask you to define God?" Bill had gone on the offense.

"Either you know God or you don't." Seneca was on the defense.

"I expected more complexity out of you Ms. Seneca."

"I think we should stop now."

"Why's that?"

"You're attacking me personally."

"I just made a casual statement."

"I feel threatened."

"I'm sorry. I guess I'll be going."

"I think that's a very good idea."

On the elevator ride down, Bill wondered where his life was really going. He had almost given up on Dorothy. His one hope was that he could mend his relationship with Sara. Of course, he knew what the psychologist would say. "That's meddling." But what the hell did they call it when they did it? Oh yeah, "therapy".

Sara and Jim were at their AA meeting.

"So, there she was. She kind of looked over in my direction. I turned back to look at the soccer players and when I turned around again she was gone. But I had a feeling that she gave me that is with me today. She must have been an angel. There's no other explanation. Pass."

The woman sitting next to Sara said, "You expect me to follow that?"

They went around the group. After they closed, Jim walked over to Sara.

"I suppose you're happy telling everyone about your angel."
"What's that supposed to mean?"
"You need to keep that private."

Sara was taken back by the comment. She quickly changed the subject, and they walked home talking about the weather.

Dorothy and Bill were home when Sara and Jim arrived.
"How was the meeting?" asked Dorothy.
"The usual," said Sara.
Jim looked down at his feet.
"I want us all to sit down at the dining room table," said Bill. "I have some news."
After they were all seated, Bill began.
"I had an appointment with a doctor today. The short and long of it is that I have dyspnea, shortness of breath."
"Oh my god," said Dorothy
Sara and Jim looked at each other in disbelief.

"The doctor thinks it's caused by stress," Bill continued. "It means I'm more susceptible to a heart attack."

"Dad, what can we do?"

"We just have to all carry on." Bill was diplomatic and collected.

"You're still going to go to court?" asked Dorothy.

"I have to. I'm too young to retire." Bill the realist.

"What does this mean?" asked Dorothy.

"I'm a fallible human being," said Bill.

"If I'm the one causing you stress, I can go. I can leave," said Jim.

"I'm not pointing fingers," said Bill. "It's just part of life."

"Part of life? Part of life?" blurted out Sara. "Why does this have to happen now?"

"God has his own timetable Sara," said Dorothy. "But, hey, no one has passed the death sentence yet."

"That's right," said Bill. "This could go on for years."

The four all looked at each other trying to stay hopeful.

"Let's go out for dinner tonight," said Dorothy.

"That sounds like an excellent plan," said Bill.

The conversation was finished.

The next day at the court building Bill was conversing with his admin.

"Dyspnea?" asked Molly.

"Shortness of breath."

"Bill, I'm so sorry."

"It's O.K. It's all right."

"Bill, I'm not going to retire."

"What? You don't have to…"

"Not with you like this."

"Molly, I don't expect…"

"Bill, I mean it. My plans can wait. I want to see you through this."

"Molly, it may end up killing me."

"One of us will go first. We'll just have to see who."

Bill went into his chambers. He looked at the docket of cases.

"Oh good, Willie Douglas will be in."

In a short while, Willie and Bill were in court with a handful of others.

"So, Willie, tell me what you've been up to."

"In what way, Judge?"

"What have you been doing?"

"The usual stuff."

"Tell me more."

"I get up at 6:30 A.M. I drink two cups of coffee, and then I make my bed. After I get dressed I take the subway over to work at the county building. I change into work clothes and start my route at 8:00. At 10:00 I take my break. I read the Bible a little, and go back to work. Then lunch. Then work. Another break. And quitting time. I go out for dinner, fast food you know. Then home. Watch a little T.V. Read the newspaper. I go to bed at 10:00 P.M. Next day the same and next day and so on."

"Well Willie. How's the reading going?"

"Tutor's been helping me, you know."

"That's amazing, Willie. And no drinking?"

"Heaven's no."

"But that fast food. Can't you upgrade?"

"They don't pay me for nothing better."

"We'll see about a raise. I'll talk to your boss. But good job Willie. Real proud of you."

"I'm proud of myself."

With that, Willie turned and exited.

Bill tried to stand up but had to sit back down to catch his breath.

God this is going to kill me yet.

While he was seated he did a little reflecting.

What did Seneca mean the other day? Sara has a sexual attraction to me? I didn't necessarily think about it that much. I just thought any such feelings were natural. Certainly not perversions or anything. Nothing that makes our family weird. What was Seneca trying to say anyhow? I'm naïve? I don't think so. My parents were square, but I never thought I was. I learned about life from Randall Smith. He was cool. Not a square. I mean I raised Sara to be cool. Popular. Liked by her friends. Where did it go wrong? Can I blame everything on mental illness? There might be doctors who would say that's O.K. "Your little girl can't be held responsible." I can hear them. At least Seneca has some expectations for Sara. I gotta too."

With that, Bill grabbed the top of the bench and pulled himself up out of the chair. When he left the courtroom, Molly was outside the door.

"Well Molly. You waiting on me?"
"Bill, Willie left ten minutes ago."
"Just doing some thinking."
"Anything you want to discuss?"
"Everything and nothing."
"What?"
"I'm wondering if my whole life is just one big mistake."
"Bill!"
"Sara. I think I failed her."
"Bill, she's got a biological illness. Mental illness is a chemical imbalance in the brain. It has nothing to do with how you raised her."
"I'm not so sure about all that. Sure, there's something going on in her brain, but I'm not sure that can't be controlled a little better. Look at the clients in mental health court. Many of them are going on to lead upstanding lives. Their brain chemistry is not holding them back."

"Everyone is different."

"What's that supposed to mean? Sara's different from the others?"

"Some people just need more time. She'll work out. I'm sure of it. How about lately? I've been hearing she's doing well."

"I wish she had never been with that Bain jerk."

"Oh him."

"What she saw in him, there's just no telling."

"Most likely not much. He probably offered excitement. Sara probably thought he was cool."

"Oh, I know that's true. But it just wasn't how we raised her."

"Haven't you ever heard of rebellion? Did your parents raise you to worship Randall Smith?"

"I didn't worship Randall Smith."

"And the alcohol she abused. Don't you think that was pretty destructive?"

"I don't have a logical explanation for it. I just feel I failed her."

"Bill…you're being hard on yourself."

"I've just got to make it up to her, make things right."

"Bill, you can't. You are her father. That's it. You've done everything you could."

"I won't be happy if I don't try."

21

"Sara? Where's Jim?"

Bill and Sara were alone in the kitchen early in the morning.

"He must not be up yet."

"How are you two getting along?"

"Fine as far as I know."

"Anything developing between you?"

"What do you mean - anything? We're kind of partners in this adventure of mental health court. We're both under your thumb."

"Sara, why do you have to say it like that?"

"It's the truth, isn't it?"

"Was I? am I? such an authority figure?"

"You've always been my father."

"What does that mean to you, Sara?"

"You always told me what to do?"

"Really? That's your perception of me?"

"Sara this. Sara that. It's how it was and still is."

"Don't you see that I have to give some direction as your father?"

"Oh, I've forgiven you."

"Forgiven me? Did I do something wrong?"

"You did the best you could."

"Sara, you're not making this easy for the both of us."

"What do you want me to say?"

"Just some kind words."

"They don't come easy, Bill."

"I always thought we had a great relationship until this mental illness happened."

"Don't you see? Can't you know? It set me free."

"Free? Is that what you think?"

Just then Jim walked into the kitchen.

"Looks like I just walked in on a big conversation," said Jim.

"No, we were just killing time. Right, Bill?"

Bill got a pained look on his face.

"Sara and I were just having a private talk, Jim."

"Well, hey, if you want me to go…" Jim looked indecisive.

"That won't be necessary, Jim. We had just finished up. Right, Sara?"

Sara took a combative stance with her body.

"Truth is, Bill and I were talking about you, Jim."

"Well, I don't know…" Jim started.

Sara jumped in. "He was asking about *us*."

Bill looked like he had been betrayed.

"Nothing personal, Jim. Curious. I was just curious."

"About Sara and me?" Jim sounded surprised. "Well we haven't slept together if that's what you mean?"

Now it was Bill's turn to be surprised.

"Heavens, we certainly couldn't have that with the court arrangements. I have to run a tighter ship than that."

"Too tight," said Sara.

Dorothy walked in.

"The whole gang is here. Wait. What's going on? You look like you were hit by a hurricane."

"Just exchanging ideas," said Bill.

"Bill's poking in our business, Mom."

"Young lady. Don't speak about your father is those terms."

"Sorry," said Sara very conscious of the tentative condition of her lodging at her parents' home.

"Now, why don't we all get some breakfast," said Dorothy.

"That would be a very good idea," said Bill.

And they sat and they ate.

When they were done Dorothy spoke up.

"Jim and Sara, I'd like you to mow the grass this morning. We won't be doing that much longer this year, but it needs it today."

"Sure, Mom," said Jim.

"I'll water the flowers and greens. It hasn't rained in a week," said Sara.

Sara and Jim went outside.

Then Dorothy looked across the table at Bill.

"What was all the commotion about?"

"Commotion?"

"Before breakfast. Sara talking about you being nosy."

"Oh, that. It was nothing."

"What are you hiding from me, Bill?"

'What do you mean hiding?"

"Only what you've done as long as I've known you."

"There are just some things you shouldn't express."

"That? Coming from a Randall Smith fan?"

"I don't think you tell me everything either, Dorothy."

"Why should I? It wouldn't be even that way."

"Are you saying I'm unfair?"

"Not always. As a judge, I think you're probably more than fair."

"But I'm not fair as a husband and father?"

"You said it. I didn't."

"We're going in circles, Dorothy."

"But zeroing in on the point."

"The point being…"

"That you are aloof and distant to your family."

"I think I'm trying to change that. That's what I was trying to do with Sara earlier."

"Wait. Here she comes."

Sara walked in.

"What do you need, honey?" asked Dorothy.

"Where's the hose?" asked Sara.

"It was in the garage unless it got moved when Jim cleaned the other week. Ask Jim."

Sara walked back out.

"As I was saying, Bill, nobody ever knew you, unless of course it was Randall Smith."

"I am trying to understand what you're saying, but you're painting a vastly different picture from how I saw it."

"Okay, Bill, tell me. How did you see it?"

"I thought we had a nice little family. I thought you loved me. I thought Sara loved me. And I thought I loved both of you."

"Go on."

"When Sara started having problems, I thought it was a brain disease. I didn't view it as a failure of the way we brought her up."

"You think so?"

"Well now you have caused me to have my doubts…about everything. Honey, do you even love me?"

"I guess I can't say. I'm not really sure. I mean I'm involved with you. I loved the man who was a lawyer and who fought for his clients. But then this mental illness stuff. It's like peering down into a bottomless well. And I think you fell in and can't get out."

"Don't you see my work as judge in the mental health court as positive? Don't you see the progress we've made?"

"But everyone there is mentally ill."

"That's exactly the type of stigma we're fighting. Having a mental illness is O.K."

"Everyone is in the muck."

"There can be recovery."

Sara and Jim came into the kitchen.

"We're done," said Sara.

"Your father and I were just finishing our conversation as well."

"Were you talking about us again?" said Sara shocking everyone.

"Sara, you don't know when to leave well enough alone," exclaimed Dorothy.

"I just speak the truth."

"That's the last thing you do, Sara. You don't know…"

"Hold on now," said Bill. "We've had enough fighting. Why do we always have to argue?"

"That's right, Dad," said Jim. "Let's talk about something pleasant."

"If you can think of anything, be my guest," said Sara.

"Winter's coming," said Jim.

"That's pleasant?" shouted Sara.

"I was making a joke, Sara. Just a joke."

"But really," started Bill. "We should be able to think of something pleasant to say. Let's try this. Let's go around the room with each person paying a compliment to the person on your left. I'll start. Jim, I think you're a fine son, and I only wish you were my biological son too."

Then Jim said, "Mom, you cook the best meals, and I'm afraid I've gained some weight since being here."

It was Dorothy's turn. "Sara, I've got high hopes for you, and I know you'll achieve all of them."

Sara screwed up her face in a scowl and said, "This is ridiculous. Something for kids."

Dorothy quickly responded, "In this house you are a kid, and you'll do what your father and I say."

"Bill, you're a good judge." Sara sat back in her chair. "Are you happy now?"

Bill was crestfallen. He knew he couldn't show this to Sara though or she'd think she had defeated him. "Fine job," said Bill instead.

"Can we go now?" said Sara.

"Where do you want to go?" asked Dorothy.

"Anywhere that's away."

Bill and Dorothy exchanged glances both knowing that Sara's rebellion had not been quelled.

The next day Sara had an appointment with Ms. Seneca.

After both women were seated, Clara began.

"How goes it, Sara?"

"Fine."

"Are you really?"

"You're the doctor. You tell me."

"What is it, Sara?"

"What is it?"

"Yes. What is wrong?"

"Nobody cares two cents what I think."

"That's where you wrong Sara. I care a lot."

"You see me because my dad pays you. That's all. I'm a paycheck."

Ms. Seneca was surprised but didn't lose her composure.

"Money is part of life Sara and we all need some. I'd like to see you try to earn some yourself."

Clara was not sure if that was too challenging.

"Oh yeah? You think I can't earn my own living?"

"Not everyone can Sara. It's O.K. if you can't."

"Truth is, I've been thinking about that...earning money."

"What are you coming up with?"

"I think I'd like to be a lawyer."

"What?"

Seneca was stunned. However, she did not want to throw Sara off balance.

"Very interesting, Sara. What gave you that idea?"

"Bill was a lawyer…before he became a judge."

"Yes, and…"

"It's more than following in my father's footsteps. I want justice." Sara summoned up her dignity. "Justice for people with mentally illness."

"Sara, this is quite a surprise. I had no idea. I mean a lawyer? That's a very very long haul."

Ms. Seneca was laying it all out there.

"It isn't really a secret, yet, you're the first person I've told."

"Where are you in school, Sara?"

"I've got my high school diploma."

Clara tried to be gentle.

"That's a start I guess. To be a lawyer though you need to get a college degree and then three more years of law school. Have you really thought about it, Sara?"

"I think I can do it."

Ms. Seneca was well aware that one of the symptoms of a mental illness is an inflated idea of oneself and what one thinks one can accomplish. Just the same Seneca was elated that Sara was motivated to do something.

"Have you made any plans?"

"Well, like you said, I'd need to go to school for four years and then choose a law school."

"You'd not only need to go to school, but you'd have to excel there, get an outstanding score on your law boards, and then do exceptional in law school. After all that you'd be lucky to get a job."

"I've thought about all that. I don't live in a vacuum you know. I know from watching my father."

"How are you and your father getting along these days?"

"Up and down. Back and forth."

"What does that mean, Sara?"

"The usual."

"Are you being coy with me?"

"You ask such dumb questions."

"Sara, come on. You're hurting my feelings."

"Then ask me something intelligent."

"I'm at a loss."

"And you're the one who is supposed to help me?"

"Sara, you've got to help yourself."

"I think I'm fine."

"Then why don't you just leave."

"OK. I'll go."

Sara got up.

"No wait, Sara. Please don't go. We need to talk."

"I'm willing."

"Sara, I don't think you have perspective on what your situation really is."

"Tell me then. What is it?"

"You're 23 years old. You've got no income. You live at home with your parents. And you've got some pipe dream about being a lawyer."

"You think it's just a pipe dream?"

"Well…?"

"I'm gonna do it. I'm gonna make it happen."

"Do you have anyone backing you on this plan?"

"Do you want to be the first one?"

"Sara. Oh Sara. What am I going to do?"

"Just believe in me. That's all."

22

Jim and Dorothy were in the kitchen.

"Sara's going to be a lawyer." Jim looked like he was delivering a bolt of lightning.

"It's about time she set a goal for herself." Instead of being shocked, Dorothy was nonplused.

"Don't you think it's too big a step for her?"

"She's got good genes. She can do anything."

"I don't know…"

"How are you going to help her, Jim?"

"I hadn't really got that far."

"Why don't you go to school with her?"

"What?"

"I can see you're no dummy. Why…"

"Maybe I could." Jim had a degree of determination in his voice. "We'd have to go to college together, then law school."

"Why sure."

"I had an 'A' average in high school."

"Now you're talking."

"There're some issues of justice where I'd like to settle the score."

"You could be my lawyer."

Bill came into the kitchen.

"Bill, Sara's going to be a lawyer."

"Is this some kind of joke?" Bill cracked a smile.

"No joke, Dad," said Jim.

Bill spread his legs out and leaned back. "That's a pretty long row to hoe."

"You did it," said Dorothy to Bill.

"I never had all the trouble Sara's had."

"Did you forget your stint on the psych ward in Boston?"

"I just don't see how it's possible."

In came Sara, and everyone got silent, and stared at her in a way that Sara could tell that they had been talking about her.

"You were talking about me?"

"Sara, I was just telling them about your aspirations," said Jim.

"Law school, Sara?" Bill tried to keep a straight face.

"It's no big deal." Sara kind of cocked her head.

"There's just a lot of work to do to make that happen, Sara, and with your past, well…"

"Don't destroy your daughter's dreams, Bill."

"I'm just trying to be realistic."

"This kind of talk from a Randall Smith devotee?"

"I thought you always said I put too much on Smith."

"This is one time you should."

Bill looked like he was outnumbered. "I guess this is cause for celebration, then."

"We should buy a bottle of wine," said Dorothy.

"Mom, you know Sara and I don't drink," said Jim.

"I meant non-alcoholic wine."

"Let's go out for dinner at the Greek House," said Bill. "We can come home to drink the wine."

"Judge Somany at Mental Health Court is going to be so proud," said Jim.

"You guys really believe me?" asked Sara.

"Of course we do," said Dorothy. "We'll start looking at schools tomorrow."

Sara and Jim were at the Methodist Church for their AA

meeting. It was Sara's turn.

"So, you guys, Jim and I have decided to become lawyers."

A woman interrupted. "I don't usually cross-talk, but I have to tell you. You don't just become a lawyer. It's years of work. Then you have to be lucky. And having a police record – it won't happen. Attempt something reasonable, something more down to earth."

Sara took a stance in her chair and said, "I've never been down to earth. Why would I start now?"

The girl kept talking, "I don't think you have the idea of the respect required for the law."

Sara returned, "I don't think I've told you this, but my father is a judge. Before that he was an attorney. I think I have a pretty good idea of what I'm getting into."

"Your father…"

The others in the group started getting restless.

Somebody said, "Let's stay on topic. The topic today is the 12th step. Tie your conversation into that."

Sara got defensive. "I'm doing just that. The 12th step tells you to practice all these principles in all your affairs. Law school is one of my affairs."

The other girl piped up, "Law school is not an affair. You seem to think it's a walk in the park. Law school is a life work."

"And I'm prepared to make it my life work."

After the meeting was over, Jim walked up to Sara.

"There you go, talking yourself into trouble again."

"What?! Why do you even think you can talk to me like that?"

"Sara, I'm trying to be your friend."

"Then say something that helps."

"If you're going to be a lawyer, you'll have to be honest."

Sara laughed. "Jim, do you know how silly that sounds? But, hey, you're right…and I can be honest you know."

"I'm not talking brutal, direct, non-flinching, honest. I'm talking integrity."

"Say, I thought you said we were in this together."

"Sara, it may be time to define our relationship."

"What for?"

"We've got to set boundaries."

"That sounds all quite boring to me."

"Sara, do you know what you sound like?"

"No. Tell me."

"You're beginning to sound like a raging lunatic."

"Good. It's a good thing I'm on medication then."

"I give up. Shall we start walking home?"

"I thought you'd never ask."

Sara and Jim walked home in their usual relative silence.

When they got home no one was around. Sara began making bedroom eyes at Jim.

"Something wrong, Sara?"

"No. Why do you ask?"

"You're looking at me quite strangely."

"Jim?"

"Yes?"

"Let's have sex."

Jim backed up three steps. "Whoa. What? Sara, are you nuts?"

"The answer is 'Yes'".

"Sara, mental illness is no joke, and for that matter neither is sex."

"Aren't you a man, Jim?"

"Sara, that isn't going to work on me. You seem to forget – we're in a program. We're clients in Mental Health Court. It's serious. All this talk of school? Is it a joke to you, Sara?"

"OK. All right, Jim. You're straight with me. I'll be straight with you. Jim, I have to know if you really care about me. I don't trust anyone unless I've had sex with them."

"How many people have you had sex with?"

"Jim, I don't want to go into it. Do you want to sleep with me or not?"

"Usually it's the male who initiates it."

"I'm waiting. Still waiting. Ask me."

Just then, they heard the front door, and in walked Bill and Dorothy.

"You two look like you've been in the cookie jar," said Dorothy.

"No, Mom, just got home ourselves," said Jim.

"While I've got some things for you to do around the house later on. Why don't you wash up for supper?"

The next day Jim and Sara were scheduled to go into Mental Health Court to meet with Judge Somany. When they arrived, the judge was in the receptionist, Molly's, office.

Maria Gonzalez and Scott Jensen showed up shortly.

"Well, everyone is here," said the judge, "Let's go into the chambers."

Once there, Somany asked Sara and Jim to approach the bench.

"It's been four weeks since you started the program. The big question is, how's it going?"

"It's going great," said Jim.

"And you, Sara? What can you share with me?"

"I'm making plans to become a lawyer," said Sara.

Somany's jaw dropped and his head fell down almost to his folded hands.

"Sara? Sara, this is most unusual. Where on earth did you ever get that idea?"

"I've always been for justice, Judge Somany."

"Everyone is for justice. Not everyone can be a lawyer. Do you have any basis for thinking that you can accomplish this feat?"

"My dad was a lawyer."

"Yes. Yes, I know. However, we're talking about you."

"It is said by many wise people that a person can do whatever she sets her mind to."

"I wouldn't want to be the person to say no to your ambitions, Sara. What steps have you taken?"

"Well it just came to me about a week ago."

"Oh. I see it just kind of occurred to you a week ago."

"That's right."

"Well, we better give it a little time to settle, don't you think?"

"You know, I'll listen to you because you're a judge and you should know."

"Thank you, young lady."

"You're welcome."

"Now you, young man, what about you?"

"I'm going to be a lawyer too."

Judge Somany's head collapsed on the benchtop. When he regained his composure he said, "So this is kind of your thing. You two are doing law school? Is it like a fad or something?"

"Oh no, Judge Somany. We are taking it very seriously."

"And you've thought about it a whole week?"

"It's just something we'd like to do as a team."

"Team spirit? That's cool."

Then Sara spoke. "I'm kind of sensing, Judge Somany, that you doubt us."

"Oh? Whatever gave you that idea?"

Sara thought she'd play along.

"So, you do believe us."

"Well…"

"That's great, Judge, because we'll need your support if we'll be successful in this."

It was Judge Somany's turn to go along with it.

"Oh yes. You have my support."

"But do we have your blessing, Judge?" asked Sara.

"Blessing? That has religious connotations, no?"

"Justice *is* very spiritual, Judge."

"Justice and the law are not the same thing," said Somany looking intently for the reaction he'd get from Sara.

"There're too many people in law who have forgotten about justice," said Sara defiantly.

"If that's so, what makes you think you'll be any different?"

"I want to make a difference. I want to bring justice back to the law."

Somany realized that such big ideas stemmed from Sara's

grandiosity which was a part of her illness. However, he

chose to meet her where she was at.

"Yes, Sara. You'll have my blessing if you can do that."

When Sara and Jim got home, Dorothy was on the computer.

"What you looking at, Mom," asked Jim.

"Just looking at schools for you and Sara. If you're going to start next September, we better get crackin'."

"I think we should be English majors, Jim," said Sara.

"You be an English major, Sara. I'll be an Econ major. You know cover our bases. You get the verbal and written skills, and I'll hold the purse with our money."

"Money. Now that brings up an interesting topic," said Dorothy. "We've got to figure a way we can finance this dream."

"I thought you and Dad would help us," said Sara.

"We can help some, but depending on the school, well, this is a lot of education we're talking about."

"Maybe we can get scholarships," said Sara.

"I don't know. Anything is possible," said Dorothy still surfing the web. "Wait, what about Berkley College right here in White Plains. And look at this. They have an on-line program."

"On-line?' asked Jim.

"Sure. Then you can do your education from home where we can still watch you. Mental Health Court will like that," said Dorothy looking further. "Oh." Dorothy stopped. "Tuition is almost $8,000 a quarter. Eight times two times three – almost 50 grand a year."

"Eight times two times three?" Sara was lost.

"Eight thousand a quarter for two people for three quarters a year unless of course you go to summer school."

"And then law school after that…well…" Jim looked defeated.

"If only we knew somebody who was rich," said Dorothy.

"About the only person we've ever been associated with is Randall Smith," said Jim.

"That's it," shouted Sara. "We can get the money from Randall Smith."

"Now how's that gonna happen," said Dorothy dejectedly.

"Bill, I mean Dad, said that Randall Smith is videotaping our lunch date. We simply sell the tape and get the proceeds." Sara looked like she had solved one of the great mysteries of the universe."

"Do you really expect Randall Smith to give us a cut of that?" Dorothy was unconvinced.

"If we make Smith look good in the video, maybe he could see his way to paying his actors." Sara was somewhat persuasive.

"It's a long shot, a long, long, long shot, but it's possible," said Dorothy. "I just don't know how we could approach Randall with this idea."

"Leave it to me," said Sara.

"Leave it to you? These things take tact and planning and connections," said Dorothy.

"I think Randall likes me," said Sara.
"LIKES YOU?!" said Dorothy.

"Well it's a start in the right direction," replied Sara.
"I just don't know how you're going to pull this one off," said Dorothy.
"I'm just going to make him an offer he can't refuse," said Sara.

Bill McCutcheon was not looking forward to this day.

Molly greeted him as usual at the elevator.

"Bill, I feel your pain."
"Molly, I'm in no mood for a joke."
"I wasn't joking."
"So, Bain Bottles is on the docket, no?"
"I'm afraid so."
"Jensen here?"
"Not yet."

Bill looked down the hall. "I'll be in my chambers." When
Bill sat down at his desk, he sighed a deep sigh. He viewed
the situation as one of fate. He coasted back in his memory.
Like everyone else he had his highs and his lows, but,
always, he had made it through. Bain Bottles presented a low
point. Bill somewhat consciously and somewhat
unconsciously blamed Bottles for the troubles that Sara now
faced. At another point in his life he may have set out to
destroy Bottles, tit-for tat, eye for an eye. But the judge part
of his life wouldn't allow that. He had to let justice take its
course. If Bottles toed the line, Bill would let it roll off of
him. Bill's present concern for Sara was greater than any
kind of revenge against Bottles. That said, it didn't come
easy. Bill fully realized he had the power to demolish Bottles.
A desire for retribution was in the picture, but Bill
suppressed it. He had never acted on such impulses and he
wouldn't let Bottles make him do so now. *No, I'm going to
stay the course. My reputation as a fair judge would preclude
me from doing something rash. If there's any mistakes to be
made, I'll let Bottles make them.*
Then Bill was interrupted by Jensen's knock on the door.
"Bill, you in there?"
"Coming out, Scott," said Bill.
In the hallway stood Scott Jensen, prosecutor, a lawyer from
the Public Defenders unit, a social worker, and, of course,
Bain Bottles. Bottles wasn't that smart, but he was smart
enough to know that if he screwed up he would be off to jail.

"Mr. Bottles, are you ready?" asked Bill.

Bain was a little surprised as if he half-expected leniency. He quickly surmised that this wouldn't be the case.

"Yes sir. I'm ready."

"Then let us proceed to the courtroom," said Bill.

"You're all business today," said Jensen.

"We'll try to keep it that way," replied the judge.

Once in the courtroom and at the bench, McCutcheon spoke, "Mr. Bottles, I set some pretty specific rules for your continued status in Mental Health Court. How have you done on these?"

Bain's social worker spoke up. "He's tried to comply with all of them."

"Let me get this straight, Mr. Bottles. You *tried* to comply on all of them."

"Yes, sir."

"I set half a dozen very specific rules for your conduct. How many of them did you *comply* on?"

"I'm not sure."

"One? Three? Five?"

"Well, I didn't do my laundry in my room."

"Wasn't that one of the rules, Mr. Bottles?"

"Yes."

"What other rules did you break, Mr. Bottles?"

"I ate some junk food."

"Once again you have broken a rule."

"Yes sir."

"Mr. Bottles, where are my written reports on your required reading?"

"I didn't do it."

"Mr. Bottles, I am forced to make a decision."

The judge looked sternly into the eyes of Bain.

"You are no longer a candidate in Mental Health Court. I hereby turn your case over to the Criminal Justice system to face the charges before you."

"Wait…Bill…" Jensen started.

"Scott, I have no other choice."

With that the judge stood up and walked towards the door.

"Judge McCutcheon, I won't do it again." Bain was pleading.

"Save it for the next judge," said Bill.

And he walked out.

Sara was in Ms. Seneca's office.

"So how are your plans for law school coming?" asked Ms. Seneca.

"I'm trying to figure out how I'm going to pay for it."

"What are you coming up with?"

"I'm planning on asking Randall Smith to pay for it."

That caught Seneca by total surprise. She rolled her eyes at the ceiling.

After a pause she spoke, "Why on earth would Randall Smith pay for your education?"

"Because I'm the Virgin Mary."

Again, Seneca was surprised. "First off, how on earth do you go on living a lie? Secondly, why the hell would anyone believe it?"

"What does it hurt, Ms. Seneca, who I believe I am?"

"Because it isn't true."

"You care about that?"

"Sara, it offends me that you think you are the Virgin Mary?"

"Don't you think you do things that offend me?"

"We're both offended by each other. That puts us at square one."

"What are you saying, Ms. Seneca?"

"Why won't you let me help you?"

"How do you see it then?"

"You have a biological/medical condition…"

"Which makes you better than me."

"I didn't say that."

"But that's where it's heading."

"How far can you get by acting on a belief that isn't true?"

"How do you know, Ms. Seneca. How do you know?"

"I know enough about your history to know you're Sara McCutcheon and not the Virgin Mary."

"Do you really think you know my Spirit?"

"How could I know your Spirit?"

"Yet you say you know I don't have the Spirit of the Virgin Mary."

"I'm saying you are not the person, Virgin Mary."

"I'm saying I have the Spirit of the Virgin Mary."

"Spiritual matters are complex. You may have her Spirit. It's possible."

"Ah ha. Then I am the Virgin Mary."

"No, you are not. There is only one Virgin Mary. You may share spiritual gifts, but that doesn't make you the same person."

"The spiritual side of life is the most important."

"I might agree."

"Then I have something pretty important that I share with the Virgin Mary."

"If you say it like that, yes, you do."

"All right then."

"But there is a whole lot of things that must fall in place before this spiritual gift can have any value to anyone."

"Don't you know what I've attained?"

"You may have attained something that you understand, but it isn't marketable. You won't make any money off it."

Seneca cast a glance that both challenged and defeated Sara at the same time. "I think we should end for the day."

23

"Bill? Randall Smith here."

"Randall, how are you?"

"Just checking in Bill. We've got, what, two weeks before our luncheon date?"

"Yes, Saturday, October 6th at 2 PM."

"And the restaurant is cool with bringing in a video crew?"

Bill realized he hadn't had Molly arrange that.

"Oh sure. Everything is set."

"I'll see you then," said Smith.

Molly was on the phone to the *New Yorker*, the restaurant having the party.

"Yes, I had an additional request for the luncheon on the patio with Randall Smith on October 6th."

"Oh?"

"We'd like to bring in a video crew to film it."

"This is most unusual. The *New Yorker* is a union workers restaurant. Will this video crew be all union workers?"

"Well, I would assume so. I mean Randall Smith…"

"We would have to see union cards."

"I'll get back to you."

Molly went into the judge's chambers, but Bill was gone. She made a decision. She felt it couldn't wait. She went into Bill's private rolodex and found Smith's number. It's something she had never done but the urgency of the situation required it.

"Mr. Smith?"

"Who's this?"

"Molly…I'm Bill McCutcheon's Admin."

"Ah huh. A friend of Bill is a friend of mine. What can I do for you?"

"It's about the luncheon."

"Yes?"

"It's about the video crew."

"Yes?"

"The *New Yorker*, the place where the luncheon is?"

"Yes?"

"They told me that the video crew has to be union workers."

"Of course they are. I would never have non-union workers."

"Oh, that's fine then."

"Say, Helen…"

"Molly."

"Molly, are you going to be there too?"

"Oh, no. Not me. I wouldn't think of invading your party."

"What? Invading our party? It would be no such thing. I want you to be there. Bill has told me all about you. Please say you'll come."

"Well…if that's what you want."

"Of course. The more the merrier."

"OK, Mr. Smith, I'll plan on it."

"See you then. Good-bye."

"Good-bye, Mr. Smith."

Molly went back to her desk to sit down. She had to analyze what had just happened. She knew she would have to tell Bill she called Smith. Then she would have to explain that she used his rolodex. What would Bill think about that?

Bill was in Ms. Seneca's office.

"So, how's it going, Bill?" greeted Ms. Seneca.

"Glad you asked." Bill took a seat. "Some things good. Others not so good."

"Let's start with the good."

"In a couple weeks, my family and I will be having lunch with Randall Smith."

"I thought we said we'd start with the good."

"Why isn't that a good thing?"

"We've been over this, Bill. Your childlike obsession with this cult figure is way out of line."

Childlike obsession? "In reality, I happen to think he is a very talented artist with a contagious message."

"What's his message? Screw the system?"

"There's a little more to it than that."

"Try me."

"Randall Smith champions the underdog. He gives the downtrodden hope. He doesn't accept "no" for an answer. Yet, he knows what it is to fail. However, he always lands on his feet."

Bill looked at Clara like he had just won a big battle.

"He sure has your soul, Bill."

"My loyalty, yes. My love, yes. But my soul? No."

"How can you be so sure, Bill?"

"What do you mean by my soul?"

"I don't know. What do you think your soul is?"

"I'm not sure I can easily define that."

"Try to."

"Jesus used to have my soul. When I was young. I was taught to give my soul over to Jesus."

"What were you giving him?"

"My soul."

"Explain."

"Do you have a couple of years?"

"Bill…"

"My deepest self. My private life that only I knew. It was a direction to go."

"Direction?"

"A call to the light."

"As opposed to what?"

"Darkness. Lying. Deception."

"So, you tried to live your life out in the open."

"The best I could."

"So how did Randall Smith figure into this?"

"Sometime in my teens I became acquainted with his music."

"And?"

"He seemed to me to be a force for the light."

"He replaced Jesus for you?"

"No. No, I wouldn't say that."

"What happened to your relationship that you had with your soul and Jesus?"

"This is all getting so deep." Bill sat up in his chair. "I would say I drifted away from thinking the Lord had my soul, and I became more interested in Randall Smith."

"Ah hah. So, Smith did get your soul."

"I don't think so... I mean...I never consciously gave it to him..."

"You sound confused."

"I became involved in my work and my family."

"Sara told me you only watched sports around the house."

"Ah Sara..."

"Yes. Let's talk about Sara."

"Has she told you she plans to become a lawyer?"

"I've told you Mr. McCutcheon that I don't discuss other clients' business with other clients."

"You're the one who said you wanted to talk about Sara."

"So, I did." Ms. Seneca gave a long glance at Bill then said, "I think she'd make a fine attorney."

"That's your job, isn't it?" Bill smiled. "To support your clients' decisions."

"When they make the right ones."

"So, you with your background in mental health and all think Sara has a chance at being an attorney?"

"I don't hold anyone back."

"I'm asking you, what are her chances?"

"I really can't say..."

"Don't be so evasive. What do you think?"

"Based on her past and the level of functioning required to be an attorney...well..;. I don't think so."

Bill straightened up in his chair.

"That's about what I think."

"But we have to let Sara try. We can't stand in her way."

"I just don't want to see her fail."

"Bill, I understand. But I do believe Sara's got the guts to fail and survive."

"I only hope you're right."

24

Sara was at Ms. Seneca's office.

"So, Sara, how are your plans for your life coming along?"

"Moving forward."

"That's it?"

"It's a big step."

"So, I'm surprised you don't want to say more about it."

"I'm building momentum."

"That's all fine and good, but can't you talk about it?"

"I'm rising to the level."

"Sara, you're being quite evasive." Ms. Seneca was concerned about Sara's mental health.

"What would you like to know?"

` "Any information you might have concerning your plans."

"Jim is ready."

"Good let's talk about Jim."

"I don't have him yet."

"What do you mean by that, Sara?"

"We haven't had sex yet."

"Is that how you *win* people over?"

"Sometimes."

"How many people have you had sex with?"

"Just one…well two."

"And they were…?"

"Bain and the fucker who raped me."

"Well I don't assume you wanted to win either of them over."

"Possibly Bain. Just because he was first. But the other numbnuts was just a bad dream."

"Sara, I don't see how you can talk so coldly about your life."

"Comes with the territory."

"What territory are we talking about?"

"Mental illness as well as being the Virgin Mary."

"Aren't the two mutually exclusive?"

"No. I think I can be both."

"Interesting." Ms. Seneca looked at her watch. "We need to stop for now."

"I was just starting to get into it."

"Sara, you've got to do some of the work on your own. I can't do it all for you."

"What do you mean by that?"

"You have to decide what's real and what's not."

"I thought that's what your job was."

"Oh Sara. Sometimes I can barely figure out my own life."

The psychologist tilted her head towards Sara and smiled. Sara tried to take in what she had just been told.

Judge McCutcheon rode the elevator up to the 15th floor to court on Friday, September 29th. Molly greeted him at the elevator.

"Your favorite is here today, Bill."

"Favorite?"

"Willy."

"Outstanding." Bill's face broke into a wide grin. "Say, is the big gig at the *New Yorker* all set for a week from tomorrow."

"Bill, Randall wants me to attend."

Bill looked at her questioningly.

"Bill, I had to call him. I confess. I went into your rolodex. I hope you forgive me this invasion of your privacy."

"Forgiven? You know I'm not uptight about things like that."

"It's just that I've always respected your position and I felt that..."

"Hey. No big deal."

"So, yes. We're all set for next Saturday." Molly paused, "Are you, Bill?"

"I believe I am." Then he said, "When Willy gets here, send him and the others into the office."

In a short while, Willy, Barnes, the case manager, Jensen, and Gonzalez were seated in the judge's chambers.

"Willy, how are you?" asked the judge.

"Fine. Fine. Mr. Judge."

"How's your program?"

"I've been good, Judge. Real good."

"Any progress?"

"I've got a girlfriend now."

"Outstanding. What's her name?"

"Delilah."

"Oh, be careful Willie. You know about the Biblical Delilah. She brought down Samson."

"My girl is fine, Judge. You leave her alone."

"What else can you tell me, Willie?"

"I'm working on Saturday now too."

"Isn't that a bit much?"

"Need the money to take Delilah out."

"Oh, I see. Sounds groovy."

"Are you disrespecting me, Judge?"

Bill was brought up short. He didn't like to think it, but on the on the other hand, he had been a little flip.

"Willy? I'm sorry."

The judge moved his head towards Willy. "I didn't mean to be disrespectful, but perhaps I was. I'll retract the statement and change it to, 'I'm happy for you and Delilah."

"Thanks, Judge. I appreciate that."

"Now, where were we?"

They talked another 15 minutes taking care of business.

Sara and Jim were at their AA meeting. Sara was cracking.

"Isn't that what you do at meetings? Let it all hang out? Come on guys. Please listen. My dad, no…my father…always wanted me to be his little girl. Wasn't I so cute? Oh, look what little Sara is doing. Oh, how pretty Sara looks today. Sara this. Sara that. It was never what I wanted. It was never what I thought. I was just an object. Put me on the shelf. Oh, so precious."

The others began to look around at each other.

"You guys, I just wanted to be normal. Normal, normal, normal."

Gertrude, one of the old-timers at the meeting, felt she had to speak.

"Sara, you're amongst friends. We all think you're great."

"What would it take my dad, father, to say that?"

Gertrude sat back. "He can't fathom what you're going through Sara. I doubt he treated you as a thing. He's what? A judge? He knows the law and that's it. Lawyers deal in money. They play games with money, not people."

"But I want to be a lawyer. Then I could get the fucker who raped me."

Everybody looked shocked.

After a seemingly endless silence, Gertrude leaned over and took Sara by the hands.

"My dear, dear Sara. You've been violated? In that way?"

Sara was inconsolable.

"Ain't no big thing. I just find the ass and shoot him."

"Sara, such words. Where does this come from?"

"Just comes with the territory."

Gertrude let go of Sara's hands.

"What territory? I would guess your upbringing was quite privileged."

"You think?" Sara puffed up her chest. "I was homeless you know."

"I'm not trying to be mean, but wasn't it of your own doing?"

"I'm sick."

"But you can recover."

"And that's just what I've been saying."

Gertrude flashed a big grin. "Then there is no problem."

Sara rolled her eyes. "Can we go on to the next person?"

When Sara and Jim walked home after the meeting both were so silent it was as though neither one wanted to give the other one a chance to get a word in edgewise.

That night they finally talked.

"You really lost it at the meeting today, Sara."

"Why are you bringing that up?" asked Sara.

"It was just a little weird and all."

"Life is weird, Jim. Get used to it."

"I mean you gotta play by the rules, Sara."

"Rules are made for small minds."

"And you want to be a lawyer?"

"The law and the rules you're talking about are two different things."

"What's that?"

"I didn't break any laws today at the meeting, but I will agree that I might have broken some society norms."

"Society norms?"

"What society expects."

"You lump all people together and call it society?"

"I learned that from Bill and he learned it from Randal Smith."

"Ah, so. You and your father do see eye to eye on some things."

"Yeah, why do you say that?"

"I observe that you and your father are basically at each other's throats and have been for a long time."

"So that's what you think, huh?"

"I mean don't you agree?"

"I guess so. But I'm trying to change."

"I wouldn't tell your dad what happened today."

"Why?"

"Your dad wants to see you doing well."

"You don't think he's competitive with me?"

"I didn't say one way or the other. I just said he wants you to do well."

"You don't think he's setting me up for failure?"

"Sara? Where do you get such ideas?"

"I think he wants me to be his little girl again."

"I think he wants you to do well."

"Which means being his little girl."

"I think he wants to fulfill his role as a father."

"And for me to be his little girl."

"He wants you to have a little character."

"Character? I'm a character all right."

"Not that kind. Someone who takes responsibility for her own life."

"Hey, I didn't ask to be born. Plus I'm mentally ill."

"If you feel you're under his thumb, you have to figure some way out."

"Then he wins."

"How so?"

"It means I didn't meet him eye to eye. I ducked him."

"Maybe you are. Is that not OK?"

"Don't you have any standards, Jim?"

"If you have to meet everybody eye to eye, I see why you want to be a lawyer."

"How's that, Jim."

"Lawyers are for equality and justice and all that."

"Oh Jim, I don't know. It's just with my father, well, it has to be eye to eye."

"And I think that's what he wants from you."

"And you think I'm up to that?"

"Yeah. Yes, I do."

"Time will tell."

Just then Dorothy called to them up in Sara's bedroom where they were.

"Dinnertime."

Sara and Jim went downstairs to the dining room, then the kitchen, but there were no signs of any dinner. Dorothy was sitting at the kitchen table reading a book.

"Mom, I thought you said it was dinnertime," said Sara.

"Why yes, it is."

"Why am I not seeing any evidence of any food?"

"Sara, I've let you and Jim slide lately. Tonight, you two are making dinner."

"What are we having?"

"Sara, you decide. That's part of the game."

In a short while Jim and Sara were thawing out hamburger, cooking noodles, and opening a bottle of Ragu sauce for the spaghetti they would be having. Sara grabbed a bag of Romaine lettuce and made four salads. Within about 20 minutes, dinner was ready.

At the table, the conversation was unfocused and a little trivial.

"Nice day today," said Dorothy. "Weatherwise."

"For the end of September, not bad," said Bill.

"I guess I'll take it," said Jim.

Sara fiddled with her food.

Then Dorothy livened the conversation.

"It's less than two weeks away."

"I've been counting the days," said Bill.

"What? You mean the Randall Smith gig?" asked Jim.

"What else?" Even Sara got in on that one.

"I mean what are we even going to say?" Jim asked the $1000 question.

"That's a good question," said Dorothy. "What about it, Bill?"

"I think we follow Randall's lead," said Bill.

"Oh you'd be good at that," replied Dorothy.

"Honey, not in front of the children," said Bill.

"Hah!" Sara couldn't be silent on that one.

"I mean Randall must have some plan," said Bill. "The whole thing is his idea."

"I for one have a couple of questions for him," said Sara.

"Sara? Are you going to be on your good behavior?" asked Dorothy.

"I just have a couple questions. That's all."

"Sara, you're not going to put Randall on the spot, are you?" asked Bill.

"I'm not saying."

Jim fumbled with his hands.

"Sara, I mean he's a star. You have to show a little decorum."

Jim as usual was trying to smooth the situation.

"The bigger they are the harder they fall." Sara smiled broadly.

"Sara, you're beginning to scare me," said Jim.

"If you can't stand the heat…"

"Just a minute Sara. Let's not make a fiasco out of the outing before it even happens. I know you will be on your best behavior," said Bill.

"I just want to know how he has this hold over your life, Bill," said Sara.

"Nobody has a hold over my life." Bill wasn't going to let Sara abuse him.

"What do you call it then?"

"Sara, I have a deep respect for the man, something it appears no one seems to comprehend. I'm just willing to stand up for what I believe, Sara. And it's not like you who make some kind of joke out of her life. The Virgin Mary? Come on."

"You think my life is a joke?" Sara looked hurt.

"I just don't understand how a grown man, a judge, of all things, can be so absorbed in one individual." Dorothy was trying to bail out, Sara.

"Are you jealous, Dorothy?"

That was the first time Bill had ever dared to say something like that.

"Low blow, Bill."

Dorothy took her fork in her left hand and her knife in her right and smacked them upright on the table in a combative stance.

"I'm glad we're getting this all out before we see Randall."

Bill was up against the wall.

"I don't think we're getting anything out, and I don't think we're making any progress."

Dorothy pushed her chair back, got up, and left.

The McCutcheon household functioned for the next two weeks. The kids did their chores, Bill went to work, and Dorothy spent most of her time trying to imagine what she was going to say to Randall Smith. It was as though they were goods on a conveyor belt getting ready to be shipped off to the restaurant called the *New Yorker*.

25

October 6 came and Bill, Dorothy, Sara, Jim, and Molly were all at the *New Yorker* at 2 PM. The maitre'd greeted them.

"How are you today?"
"Party for Randall Smith," said Bill proudly.
"Why yes. Please follow me."
The headwater led the group through several rooms, past the bar, and out to the patio. The temperature was a brisk 55 degrees, but it was sunny. There was one table set for six. Of course, Randall was not there yet. However, the video crew was. It consisted of a cameraman, a sound tech, and a director.

"Hi," said the director. "You must be Bill McCutcheon," he said addressing Bill.
"Yes. Yes I am."
"Let's get you set up with mics."

The director motioned to the sound man who had five mics that he fit unto each of the guests.

As everyone got situated, Sara suddenly blurted out, "Where's Randall?"

The director cast a sheepish grin and said, "Mr. Smith is known to be late."

Everyone smiled a knowing smile. They just stood there for about five minutes which seemed like a couple of hours. Then, just as in the movies, Randall was there. He walked right over to Bill.

Randall had aged since his big star days, but his skin still shone, although he was mostly gray. But his eyes had not lost their fire.

"Bill, how the heck are you?"

"Fine, Randall, fine." What else could he say?

"Won't you introduce me around?"

When Bill got to Sara, Randall exclaimed, "Oh, yes. I remember our little talk when you weren't doing so well," referring to a past conversation he had had with Sara when she was mostly in a psychotic state.

"I'm doing much better now," popped Sara.

"Oh, my. I guess so," said Randall.

"Mr. Smith, here is your mic," said the sound tech.

"Let me get this…O.K., when do you want to start shooting?"

"You're the boss, Mr. Smith."

"Ah yes," said Randall. "Just so you folks know, this is going to be live."

The others looked somewhat shocked.

"Adds to the excitement," said Smith. "It will be right on my webpage."

Sara smiled to herself. It was all fitting into her plan.

"O.K. Let's launch it," said Smith, and the crew began filming.

"All right. Won't everyone take a seat."

The maitre'd directed Smith to the head of the table with Bill to his right and Dorothy to his left. Sara and Jim sat on Dorothy's side of the table, and Molly sat next to Bill.

"What are we having to drink?" the headwaiter asked.

Smith ordered a beer, and the rest all had sodas.

"So, Bill. Won't you tell the audience a little about our history?"

The waiter brought the drinks and told them they would all be having the same thing to eat – New York strip, green beans, and garlic mashed potatoes.

"Sure, Randall."

Bill sat back in his chair and looked up to the sky.

"I became aware of you sometime in my eighth-grade year in Junior High. You had just started. You had a record out, and some of your songs were on the radio. I can't say you immediately captured my full attention…"

"I didn't?" said Smith laughing.

"I just thought you were O.K.…interesting…I thought you were interesting."

"That's not all bad. Interesting, huh?" said Smith again laughing.

"But then something happened my sophomore year in high school. I asked the prettiest girl to dance at a party, and she rejected me. It hurt my pride. But I really discovered you."

"How so?"

The waiter brought the meals.

"You sang about disappointments in life. You talked about rejection. I had thought rejection made me a leper, but you were a star. You made me feel like I was going to be all right."

"Well, that's quite a tribute."

"Wait there's more to the story. You continued to teach me things that I couldn't learn elsewhere."

"What was I teaching you?"

"You were educating me."

"I hope I was teaching you the right things."

"You taught me feelings were important, not only my own, but others too. It was the love."

"Oh yeah?"

"And the knowledge. You thought all knowledge is valuable."

"Sometimes knowing something hurts."

"Doesn't mean it's not worth knowing. Sometimes learning is a painful process."

"Yes. That's true."

"The knowledge you taught brought me pain sometimes."

"You seem to say all knowledge is good."

"I think so."

"Even knowledge of evil things?"

"Evil is a vacuum. It just keeps sucking you in, not teaching or giving you anything. But if you don't know evil, you don't know good."

"I taught you all that?"

"You were a figurehead. Someone to bounce ideas off of. Before I ever met you."

"I guess I've heard that before, but I don't really know how I did that."

"I think it's because you didn't compromise the truth. You sought the truth. No holds barred."

"Well, thank you, I guess."

"We better let the others talk. We're dominating the conversation."

"We're just fascinated by it all," said Molly.

"It's what I've been hearing all my life," said Dorothy.

Jim and Sara had nothing to say.

"You two kids are pretty silent," said Randall finally.

"We're from a different era," said Jim. "It's kind of difficult to relate."

"I can and do relate," said Sara. "I just don't know if I believe it all."

"Whoa. What do you mean by that, Sara?" asked Smith.

"You said a lot of things in your songs that I find hard to believe you really meant it."

"Sara, shut your mouth," snapped Dorothy.

"No, no. Let Sara here have her say," demanded Smith.

"But Randall, this is live," interjected the judge.

"All the more reason to have Sara given a chance to speak her mind."

Smith sat back in his chair and gave Sara his full attention.

"There's just a lot of stuff you said that I don't think you meant."

Sara leaned forward in her chair, her hands folded and on the table.

"Oh, you're familiar with my art?"

"Growing up as Bill's daughter how couldn't I be?"

"Do you have any examples of things I'd said that you don't think I meant?"

"Randall, no one can take 100% responsibility for everything they've ever said, It's not human."

Bill was panicking.

"Sshh, Bill. I want to hear what Sara has to say." Then once again giving his attention to Sara, Smith said, "Give me an example or two to back up your claim, Sara."

"You have repeatedly said you back up the underdog."

"You don't think I meant that?"

"I just don't see any times you have done this." Sara stuck out her chin and fluttered her eyes.

"Sara, my whole life had been one of fighting for the underdog."

"You say this, but how have you ever done this?"

"Sara, what do you want from me?"

"The proceeds from sales of this video."

There was a long moment of silence at the table.

Finally, Dorothy practically shouted, "Sara, are you out of your mind?"

"Let Sara be." Smith was un-rattled. "How did you come to make such a request, Sara?"

"I'm an underdog."

"And you think I should support you financially."

"Money talks. Words are cheap."

"Sara, I don't think my words are cheap."

"Then back them up."

"Sara, the funny thing about taking someone at their word is that the other one can take you for your word as well."

"So…?"

"First off, I want to know what you'll do with the money."

"Jim and I are going to further our education."

"Oh? Get a college degree?"

"And law school too."

"Well Sara, if we're going to have an agreement we would have to have a contract."

The maitre'd interjected, "Shall I get pen and paper?"

Smith quickly said, "No. We have it on film."

Sara asked, "What are your terms?"

"You must complete – both of you – must complete the full education. If you don't, you must pay all the money back."

"That's pretty strict terms," said Sara.

"I'm not done. You must maintain an "A" average…A- is O.K."

"Wow, you're tough."

Smith sat back and grinned. "Do we have a deal or not?"

Jim and Sara took a long look at each other, gritted their teeth, and said, "O.K. Deal."

"Well, there you have it folks in video land. Do words still matter? I say they do."

Bill looked disturbed. "Surely, you're not going to do this, Randall."

"Bill, you helped out in that legal jam I was in a few years back. I owe you."

"But you paid your legal bills, Randall. I mean this is straight out of the blue, big sky!"

"Hey, I took a risk to be here today. This is what can happen when you take a risk."

Randall looked over at Sara, and Sara looked right back at Randall.

Jim said, "Hopefully your fans will approve."

"Just as long as they don't all think I'll put them through school."

Everybody, even Dorothy, laughed.

Then Randall said, "But there's more to the contract."

"We already have a deal," said Sara.

"We didn't shake on it yet," retorted Smith. "I want to have a vote on what type of law you'll practice."

"How can we know that now?" asked Jim.

"Tell me a little about your interests."

Jim started, "I'm very concerned about climate change."

"And you Sara?"

"I'm concerned about those who are affected by mental illness. I believe in the Fairweather Model of recovery."

Randall said, "Then it's easy. Jim, you'll be an environmental lawyer, and Sara, you'll advocate for the Fairweather Model of recovery."

"Well, it's settled," said Sara.

"Not yet," stated Smith. "Neither one of you can make more than $50,000 a year. Anything over that goes to charity. I'll take your word on that."

Sara looked overwhelmed. "Anything else?" asked Sara meekly.

"No. I think it's a good deal. Why don't we shake hands on it."

Smith, Sara and Jim all stood up. Then Randall facing the camera said, "As you can see, I am a man of my word." He shook Jim's hand, then Sara's.

The people at the party had not even eaten their food.

Molly said, "Why don't we eat?"

Smith replied, "I do business better on an empty stomach, but now that we're done with business, I agree. Let's eat."

26

Sara was with Ms. Seneca.

"Sara? Are you serious? Randall Smith is going to pay for your education?"

"Well, he made some rules about it, but, yes, he is going to finance Jim's and my education?"

"Sara, I know you can't twist the arm of a man like Smith easily…"

"There was no arm twisting."

"How then? He didn't just do it out of the goodness of his heart."

"To the contrary. That's exactly why he did it."

"You're naïve."

"And you're cynical."

"If he gives you money, he has to give it to everyone."

"No, that's not true."

"Why you and not somebody else?"

"I took the risk. It was my idea."

"You're so great?!"

"Not really. But Smith is."

"What I'm not getting is the why."

"He's got high standards, and I made him live up to them. I just said that if you're really for the underdog you'd do this for me. And he said, O.K."

"It's a dream. A total dream."

"And I'm living it."

"I'll believe it when I see your diploma."

"That could be a while. My mother is looking into schools now, though."

"So, Smith is giving you the money, I never…"

"He's not just opening up his bank account. Jim and I are getting the proceeds from the video we made at the restaurant. In a sense, we're just paid actors."

"Sara, it's about time you had a little luck."

"It's not luck. It's justice."

"However, you want to think about it. I'm just happy for you."

Sara and Jim were at their AA meeting. It was Sara's turn.

"So, I'm getting the impression that a lot of people do not think Jim and I can do law school. My parents have doubts, my therapist has doubts…"

The same girl who questioned Sara about law school several weeks earlier, broke in, "I don't want to interrupt you, Sara, but I do think it's for your own good, I mean, don't you think it's O.K. that people have their doubts?"

"I don't have any doubts. Why should others?"

Jim looked up at the ceiling unable to meet Sara's gaze.

The girl said, "It isn't natural to have no doubts."

"Jesus didn't."

"Are you claiming you're Jesus?"

"No."

"Well that's good…"

"The Virgin Mary."

"How can we take you as serious?"

"The only thing required for AA membership is a desire to not drink. Third tradition. Look it up."

"Honesty is the bedrock of AA."

"Who's being dishonest?"

"I give up. Go on with your little charade."

"So, as I was saying, everyone doubts me. It's pretty tough when no one believes you. All I want is someone to have faith in me."

Jim took a risk and said, "I have faith in you, Sara."

"You don't count. You're in this with me. I need somebody else, besides you, Jim, who believes in me."

Jim took another risk, "Maybe Randall Smith does."

Sara looked surprised, but her eyes lit up.

Jim went on. "He's paying for your education, isn't he?"

The AA meeting was breaking up into a free-for-all.

"Randall Smith is paying for your education?"

Sara lifted up her head, "That's what he says."

"Your Higher Power must be with you."

Sara looked around, "That's what I've tried to tell you guys."

Somebody else, "Can we return this to an AA meeting?"

Jim said, "A very good idea."

After the close of the meeting, Jim and Sara were outside the church.

Jim said, "I don't know if Randall Smith would like it that you're telling everybody."

"It's publicity for him, Jim."

"He may want his kind works to be more private."

"On the contrary. I think he relishes the spotlight."

"He likes a microphone when he's singing, but…"

"Don't be absurd. It's all part of the package."

"So, you think it's all marketing to him, huh?"

"Jim, don't be so naïve. He has an image to protect. That's all."

"Don't you think he has any sincerity?"

"Oh, I suppose he does. I just don't think it drives him."

"What drives him, Sara?"

"Applause, headlines, galas in his honor."

"I like to think he really believes in his message."

"I don't know. Maybe you're right. But his message has changed over the years, too, Jim."

"Doesn't make it any less important to him."

"Hey, we got the money. Why analyze it?"

"He set some parameters, Sara."

"He can't just let go that kind of money without any attachments."

Just then Sara's phone rang; Jim left.

"Hello, this is Sara."

"Well, Mr. Smith, this is a surprise."

"Oh. You got my number from Bill."

"You've got bad news?"

"The deal's off?"

"Your financial people won't go for it?"

"What are you saying? We had a deal on live TV."

"There was no written contract?"

"How about our verbal agreement?"

"Verbal agreement. That's all it was. Not enforceable."

"Oh, yes it is."

"How do you know?"

"I thought you'd say that so I looked it up."

"You would make a good lawyer after all. Say, let me get back to you on this."

"You've got a week."

"Wait a minute, lady. Do you know who you're talking to?"

"Someone who won't keep his word?"

"You will make a good lawyer indeed. Bye."

"Jim, Smith called me. He tried to bail."

Jim and Sara were in the Tudor mansion in the kitchen on a morning the next day.

"It's a dream, Sara. I knew he'd never follow through."

"Hold you horses. Not so fast. He pretty much indicated he'd think about it."

"You think Smith tells the truth?"

"He's made a life out of saying he does."

"It's just not how things are done."

"What do you mean?"

"You should have to work to get money."

"Oh yeah?"

"Yes. People get jobs. They earn their living."

"Not everyone."

"Most."

"So, what are you saying?"

"Give it up."

"Give up on the idea of getting an education?"

"No. Don't give that up. Just figure out a way to finance it some other way."

"Maybe I should become a prostitute, huh? What about that?"

"Sara, don't start with me."

"It's just that I don't know any other way than Smith."

"Use your imagination, Sara."

"I'm at a loss."

"You'll think of something."

"Jim, you're right. I'm going to call back Smith and tell him I don't want his money."

"You don't have to say it like that. Be business-like."

"That's it!"

"What?"

"I start a business to finance our education. I'll just have to think of what it will be."

Sara was on the phone with Smith.

"So, you see Mr. Smith, it's just not right."

"Well, we had a deal…"

"It's not the proper way to go about things, and I'm letting you off the hook."

"I've got my pride. I don't make a habit out of going back on my word."

"I don't doubt that. But, please. See it my way. I have my pride too."

"O.K. O.K But what of the video?"

"I'm going to leave that up to you."

Sara and Jim were up in Sara's bedroom during the afternoon.

"Jim, have you got any bright ideas about what kind of business we can go into?"

"We have got to avoid student loans."

"I hear that. Mom says we need $50,000 a year."

"That's a full-time job and then some."

"What about scholarships?"

"We could try I guess, but I don't know how we'd qualify."

"It's obvious that we need a job. If we both make $25,000…"

"What skills do we have?"

"What about sales?"

"Jim, that's a great idea. We'll go into sales."

"What do you want to sell?"

"How about houses?"

"Sounds like a plan."

"Sara, we're awfully good planners, aren't we?"

"The best."

27

"You're going to sell houses? Be real estate agents?"

Judge Somany was just not surprised anymore about the ideas of Sara and Jim.

"We might have to work days and go to school on-line or at night," said Sara.

"It's the only way we can pay for our education," said Jim.

"You'll have to get licenses."

The judge leaned back in his chair behind his desk in his chambers.

"How do you know you'll be able to sell?" asked the judge.

"We sold you, didn't we?" smiled Sara.

"You've got spirit young lady. That's for sure. I'm just worried you're biting off too much."

"The Virgin Mary raised a savior, didn't she?"

"Are we back to that idea, Sara? Which Virgin Mary are you talking about anyway?

"I don't want to discuss it."

"You're the one who brought it up."

Jim intervened. "It's something we'll work on together, Judge Somany."

"Well, I give you two credit. You aren't afraid to take on challenges."

"It's our beliefs," said Jim.

"Tell me more."

"Most people think Sara's ideas are whacko, but they really stem from compassion."

"How's that."

"To put it right up front: Sara loves Jesus."

It could have gone a number of ways, but Somany took the comment seriously.

"I'm happy you do, Sara."

"It's the Light. It's a battle for the Light." Sara was solid with determination.

"That has a pretty long history, young lady."

"I'm trying to make room for Christ to return."

"That's all good I'm sure."

"It's what I'm about."

"And what does your father say about all this?"

"What does he have to do with anything?"

"What is your relationship with your father?"

"We don't really see eye-to-eye."

Somany grimaced and said, "Yes, I think that's true."

"I'm trying to make my own way."

"Nobody can help you?"

"I guess I've tried. When you've been homeless and the whole world turned its back on you, you realize that it's really up to you. Doesn't mean you don't trust people anymore or that you don't believe others are trying to help; it just means you don't rely on that kind of help."

"What kind of help are you talking about? Sounds like you don't believe in love or something like that."

The comment threw Sara off guard and the judge sensed it.

"What I mean is, you don't want to let people in your life." Somany was trying.

Sara looked down, and Somany realized that probably wasn't the right approach either.

"What I'm trying to say is that you're doing a good job with your life."

Sara said, "Thank you, Judge Somany. I needed to hear that."
The judge looked over to Jim.

"And you, young man, what do you have to say for yourself."
"I'm just trying to support Sara the best I know how."
"And how do you do that?"
"I try to support her decisions."
"Even the Virgin Mary thing?"
The judge wondered if he had said the right thing, but it was too late.
"I suspend judgement," said Jim, fully realizing he was speaking to a judge who made a life out of judging people.
"You don't think about it?"
"Oh, I think about it. It just causes me to have questions more than reactions."
"How's that?"
"How could anyone but Sara know if she has some kind of relationship with the Virgin Mary?"
"But she says she IS the Virgin Mary?"
"When one goes on with a relationship, boundaries get broken down. People share identities."
"It's a boundary thing?"
"The psychiatrists would say Sara has a boundary issue. They say Sara is not herself. I see Sara as having enhanced boundaries to be able to identify with someone with the stature of The Virgin Mary. Almost seems sacrilegious to be talking about it this way."
"Yes."
"But you get used to it after having been in the mental health system with all the probing questions."
The judge smiled. "If you go to law school you'll have many more questions coming at you."
Jim cast back his head and said, "I think we can handle it."
"Sounds like you'll defend her to the death."
"I just might, Judge."
"Well, what can I do for you two?"
"Keep us on the right side of the law?" said Jim.
"That's something you have to do for yourself, young man. Keep your integrity."

"Well, we've been pretty good lately," said Sara.

"And I commend you. You should be proud of yourselves."

"We'll be proud when we pass the bar exam, Judge."

"I'll let you go then, and the best to you," said Judge Somany.

Sara was talking at an AA meeting.

"So the thing I value the most in my life is stability."

Some of the eyes in the room rolled, but Sara ignored it.

"I realize I was highly unstable even within the last year. With all that's gone on it's no small wonder."

"What are you talking about Sara? You've been living with your father."

The commenter looked and asked in exasperation.

"That's exactly what I mean," said Sara. "My father and I don't communicate well. A lot of stuff goes unsaid. There're skeletons in the closet. My mother tries to open my father up, but he stays tight as a drum. It made me nuts for quite a while, but now I'm beginning to see the light. He thinks like a lawyer. He is everyone's adversary. On the surface he's a nice guy, but on a gut level, well, he's a fighter. He fights every day. But I can use that to my advantage. I can learn to fight him back. Up to now, I've just had a big mouth, and it's been at his throat and heart. I'm learning, though. And the best way I can fight my father is to be successful. And you know what? That's what he has always wanted. So I'm focused on him like a scientist looking through a microscope. I just can't make one false move."

"Don't you think you're taking this a little far?" The commenter spoke again.

"I've just begun," said Sara.

As they were walking home, Jim acted like it was sunny and 75 degrees even though it was grey and 50.

"Sara, I'm so proud of you," said Jim.

"Really Jim?"

"What you said made a lot of sense to me," Jim said.

"I'm 23 years old, Jim and I think I've finally figured out my dad."

"How's that, Sara?"

"Like I said in the meeting. He thinks like a lawyer. To him life is one big competition. We're all adversaries of each other. When he was young, he got a message, mostly through Randall Smith, that he could believe in. He took the word from Smith, just like my mother said, and he turned it into his own battle for justice. Being a judge has offered him an opportunity to gain some fidelity to Smith's message. So, he's all set. I don't have to worry about him anymore."

"What's this 'worry about him' all about? I just see you yelling at him."

"Because it's the only way I can express my love to him. I don't dote on him, no. But I am passionate about him. I've been very touched by his work with the Mental Health Court."

"Sara, I've never heard you talk this way."

"Because I didn't understand myself, Jim."

"And the Virgin Mary thing?"

Sara looked startled. "It's who I am, Jim."

Jim didn't respond right away. He wanted Sara to hear her own words.

Then he said, "I only see you as Sara." He looked into her eyes.

"Sara's dead. She doesn't exist anymore." Sara was starting to get agitated.

"How about this, Sara? You are still Sara, but you are the new Sara."

"I don't know, Jim. I really feel that God is calling me to be the Virgin Mary. It's just the idea that's been planted in my brain."

"Tell me more."

"Like you know, I was on the playground and taking some abuse from a loudmouth girl. I felt myself sinking. Then I looked over to the sidewalk nearby. An old lady looked at me and smiled."

"That's it? That's all it was?"

"Let me continue. I felt a strange warmth in my heart. I looked back at the loudmouth girl. Then I looked back to the sidewalk. There was no old lady."

"She probably just turned off the sidewalk."

"She couldn't have done it that fast, Jim. No, she was an angel."

"Maybe she was. But how do you become the Virgin Mary through her?"

"It was just like the angel who talked to the Virgin Mary in the Bible."

"Wait. If you're the Virgin Mary, then who was that back in the Bible?"

Sara hesitated. Then she said, "That must have been me in the Bible."

"But you live in the 21st century, over two thousand years have passed."

Sara looked a little stumped. "Don't get technical with me, Jim."

Sara looked right on edge.

Jim realized he better stop pushing her. He knew it was difficult for her. He had his own problems. Better to drop the subject.

"Look at that house." Jim pointed over to a purple house.

"That's different," said Sara.

"We'll be selling houses like that, Sara."

"I don't think we'd make much of a commission on that one, Jim."

"You can't judge a book by its cover, and you can't judge a house by its color. You have to look at its potential."

"Ms. Seneca, my therapist, told me sometimes you have to call a spade, a spade."

"Don't tell that to a black person."

Sara looked offended. "You're too weird."

"That's what my shrink says."

"Jim?" Sara was serious.

"Yes?"

"Do you really think we can sell houses?"

"It will be a piece of cake. College, then law school, will be a little tougher."

"We'll make it won't we, Jim."

"Ya know what? We're starting to become a team."

"We're just friends, Jim. Nothing more. Don't try to read something into it that isn't there."

Jim looked a little hurt. "I…was…n't. I..was…just…saying."

"Friends, Jim. We're just friends."

"O.K. All right then.

They were silent for a period of a few minutes.

Then Sara said, "I think we should research, Jim, about becoming realtors on the web."

"Sounds good. I imagine you just get a license and join a company."

"Sure. There's probably nothing to it."

"Right. Easy as pie."

"How about easy as the Hudson River."

"Whatever."

28

Jim and Sara were at the computer.

"So, it looks like we'll need 75 hours of class as a first step to become real estate agents," said Jim.

"The class is going to cost money, Jim, and we have none."

"Just as long as you don't intend us to get money like we tried when you were homeless."

Sara laughed. "No, I'm all about legitimacy now, Jim."

"We could try to get part-time jobs. Our expenses are minimal. We could save the money up fast."

Sara said, "I wonder if our Fairweather Program would get us a job?"

"We got kicked out, remember?"

"Sometimes they still help with jobs in the community."

Sara was on the phone.

"Hi Lisa."

"Sara, is that you?"

"Yes. It's me. What I was wondering is whether you could help Jim and me find a job."

"Wait a minute. Hold on. What's going on?"

"Jim and I are going to law school, but first we're going to get college degrees. In order to pay for that we are going to be real estate agents. Right now we're trying to get a job to pay for a required class in order to be agents."

"Sara, you've been away from the lodge almost a year. What makes you think I'm going to help you find a job?"

"It will look good for the program. Successful grads and all that."

"You didn't really graduate from the program, Sara."

"I don't want to get caught up on technicalities. Are you going to help me or not?"

"There're some hoops you and Jim have to jump through first, Sara."

"I figured."

"Meet me at the Lodge 7:30 tomorrow."

"PM?"

"AM"

Sara and Jim were at the Washington Lodge.

"So, Sara, if you have a valid license, I know of a job as a delivery person for Amazon."

"Yes, I could do that."

"And Jim, you were never formally kicked out of the Lodge. I could bring you back on the janitorial crew."

"That'd be great. But the worksite is not accessible by mass transit."

Lisa looked at Sara. "Would you have access to a car?"

"I think Bil...my dad, would let me use his under the circumstances."

Lisa looked relieved. "You would take Jim to and from work. You would need to fix your schedule for Amazon around that."

"Could be done, yes."

"It's settled...that is if you pass the interview at Amazon."

Sara was at the Amazon warehouse in New Jersey.

"You see Miss... Miss McCutcheon, we are not able to offer you a driving job because we see you had an offense with a stolen car."

"I was found innocent."

"Our records show you were arrested for auto theft."

"And found innocent."

"Were you arrested?"

"Yes, but..."

"I'm sorry, Miss McCutcheon..."

"Could you offer me any job, anywhere?"

"You say you were innocent? Well, we have a night shift from Thursday through Sunday, 6:00 PM through 6:30 AM in the warehouse. Would that do?"

"Yes. Yes. I'll take it."

Sara and Jim were at home.

"Jim, I just realized something. We don't even know how much the real estate class will cost."

"Oh my God. That's true. Time to go to the computer."

They googled "Real Estate Agent Training Cost".

Sara burst out laughing, "$150. We went to all that trouble to get jobs and everything for a lousy $150."

"Well, I guess we won't be working long."

The judge and Dorothy came through the front door.

Dorothy asked, "What are you kids up to?"

"Mom, Sara and I got jobs so we can pay for real estate training classes so we can sell houses."

After Dorothy's eyes shot up to the ceiling, Sara and Jim

explained their plans.

It was Tuesday, November 6, 2012, election day. When the returns came in later that night, everyone in the McCutcheon household was happy Obama won. There was a double celebration: the re-election of the president and kids' new jobs. Sara started on Thursday and Jim started Monday, the 11th.

Sara was on the road. The trip would take an hour and a half to get from White Plains to Carteret, NJ where the Amazon plant was. This was the first job she'd had in a while so she was a little nervous. But everything had been discussed in the interview. The employer knew about her connection to the Washington Lodge and that Sara was diagnosed with a mental illness. So, Sara knew that there was nothing to be nervous about yet she couldn't help but feel a little anxious. It would go away once she started working she thought.

Sara arrived at the plant, parked the car, and went in the entrance marked "Employees". She was met by Bob, a foreman, who seemed like a nice guy. He showed her around and then started her on a project. She was assigned to do inventory, first on paper, then transferred onto the computer. By 7:00, an hour later, she was no longer feeling anxious and was actually enjoying herself. The room was noisy but they gave her earplugs. By 8:00 it was time for her first break.

Sara chitchatted with some co-workers, went back to work, and finished at 6:30 AM. She could barely keep her eyes open as she drove home, and she wondered if she could last at Amazon.

As she came through the front door of her house, she was greeted by her mother.

"How's the working girl?" smiled Dorothy.
"Beat." Sara barely looked at her mother and headed to bed.
The next day, the same thing.
When she got home she said to Dorothy. "I think selling houses will be easy compared to this."

By Monday morning, Sara could finally smile. But she couldn't really sleep too long because she had to take Jim to his janitor job at 3 PM to get there by 4 PM. She'd hang out in the break room and read while Jim was working, then take him home. Jim was just scheduled to work Monday through Wednesday because Sara could only drive for those days.

On Wednesday morning, Sara was seeing Ms. Seneca.

"So I have this job now, Ms. Seneca."
"That's fabulous. Where do you work?"
Sara told her about her first week on the job and how it was only temporary until she and Jim could sell houses.

"You've got some big dreams there young lady."
"Bill always taught me to think big."
"Speaking of your father, how is it going between you two?"
"No changes there."
"Isn't he proud that you're now working?"
"I guess so."
"There's not much communication between you is there?"
"That's how I like it."
Ms. Seneca winced. "Can't you talk to your father, Sara?"
"When I was a young girl, he always gave his little commands like he was giving me a mission. Now I'm on it. I respect him, but there is nothing close between us." Sara couldn't hide her sorrow.
"Sara? What's wrong?"
"Nothing. No, nothing."
"Sara, won't you tell me?"
"You said we were going to burn my past. Remember?"
"I may have said that in the heat of the moment, but…"
"I don't feel my dad's love."
"Wow." Ms. Seneca leaned forward. "That's pretty deep."
"I'm not sure I ever will."
"Explain that to me."

"From the time I was a little girl, I thought I knew my dad. And I thought we loved each other. Then when I met Bain he turned me against my father. Bain made my father look square."

"Square?"

"Out of touch." Sara began to tear up. "Bain convinced me that my father didn't care about me. AND I BELIEVED HIM. Now…now there's been so much damage done…I just don't know how to repair it all."

"Don't you think your father forgives you?"

"I just don't know if I can feel it in my heart."

"Maybe if you're waiting for a special feel to things…well it might not happen. In many ways life is a solo journey. We can only get so much love from someone else."

"I thought things would improve at one time. I met with Randall Smith and he made me make some kind of reconciliation with my dad. But then with Bain and all…well, my dad and I just took to fighting."

"Don't you think your dad was fighting for your love too?"

"Fighting for my love?"

"Don't you think he needs your love too?"

"He's got everything. What does he need?"

"The need for love is never quenched. We all need. Especially, your dad needs your love."

"My dad?"

"Your dad."

"I thought I always did love my dad."

"You're not a girl any more. Your dad is probably looking for something more."

"More?"

"I think you know what I mean. It's stretching your mind and communicating feelings that come from within."

"Really."

"You're the one who said you wanted a love to grow between you and your father."

"I just don't know how to do it."

"Nobody does really. We all guess."

"That's what I'm doing with my Virgin Mary thing. I'm guessing a lot."

"Sara, don't go there. Sara McCutcheon is perfectly fine and capable. You don't need to be somebody else."

"But it's like you said. It's more."

"Try to discover the real Virgin Mary. What's she like? What can she communicate?"

"This is all very hard."

"I didn't say it would be easy."

"I just want to be accepted."

"Then you need to give people a reason to accept you."

"You mean like be kind to them or something."

"Yes."

Ms. Seneca looked at her watch.

"Let's end for today, Sara. But, hey, great session. Maybe our best yet."

29

Bill was in seeing Ms. Seneca.

"Sara said that?"

"She really wants your love."

"I always thought I gave that to her."

"THAT? Is that what you call love?"

"You know I'm getting it from all sides, but it's all the same message: I don't love people."

"Now you're being the extreme one. I didn't say you didn't love Sara. I don't doubt you do. But it's the singer not the song."

"What's that?"

"A great song can be destroyed by a bad singer. And, just the same, a bad song can be pretty good with the right delivery."

"So it's my approach to love?"

"I don't even know if you have an approach at all."

"OK. I'm going to level with you. I think the mental health system screwed my life up."

"Oh my God. You're blaming me?"

"The mental health system told me at a young impressionable age that I was sick, didn't measure up."

"Did someone say that to you?"

"Yes. My doctor at that time told me, and I must say, much the same as you, that my love of Randall Smith was childish and not right."

"You seem to think it's OK. Why would you let anyone stop you from liking a particular artist?"

Bill fell back in his chair.

"Only because you and so many others have told me it's a failing affair. But I've always seen it differently. Loving Smith was not a candy cane licking event. Sure, I felt the pain he evoked. It probably even made me a little sick. But anyone with any sense of the world knows the bad. I just didn't want to put on rose colored sunglasses and not look. I used the knowledge I learned from Smith to make a fight for justice, and in some small way I've done that."

"In some small way? Maybe it just hasn't been enough."

"We all fall short. I don't accept everyone singling me out. Everyone else is pointing the finger before it's pointed at them. Look, I'm willing to take responsibility. I always have. But there are some things that are impossible."

"Never say something's impossible if you haven't tried it."

"Oh, I've tried."

"Everything?"

"You want me to give Sara everything?"

"She's your only daughter. It's not like you have to divvy yourself up."

"Do you know what you're asking?"

"Do you want your daughter's love bad enough?"

"Give her everything, huh."

"Do you even know how?"

"I've given it all to someone before you know."

"Randall Smith?"

"Afraid so."

"Well, summon it all up and give it your best."

"I'm just thinking how to do it."

"Just do it. Don't think about it."

"That's where you're wrong Ms. Seneca. This will require all the thought I've got in me."

Bill sat on the train. *Sara was such a good little girl. Thought of others. Did well in school. I thought she would have a great adult life. Things went awry when she met Bain Bottles. I hope he never gets out of jail. But even though he's out of the picture, Sara and I still aren't right. Sara and I aren't right? Let me think. Did I make her a Daddy's girl? No man could replace me so with Bain she didn't even try? She was ripe for picking? I should have punched Bain in the nose. Wait. Sara should have done that. Jim seems like a nice boy. I wonder if Sara likes him. How do I proceed? Do I give the relationship my blessing? Does Sara even need me to do that? I think she is dependent on me, and she might even be angry that she is. I don't think she knows she is. How do I get her to be dependent on Jim? Maybe the AA way of no dependence on others is right for Sara. Maybe she doesn't need dependence on someone. But she is dependent on me. Everyone has her needs. Can I make it OK to let Sara be dependent on me and then shift her over to Jim? Sara's running hurt. Doctors say it's mental illness. Seems to me she not getting her needs met. Does she want to get her needs met? She's been so rebellious. Oh. My stop.*

"I just don't want to be a burden to anyone." Sara was talking to Jim in the kitchen on a Wednesday morning.

"Sara, you're no burden. Where did you get that idea?"

"I just see how people react to me. It looks like their eyes are sinking into their mouths."

"You can't be so sensitive about it."

"But I am sensitive. I do notice."

"What can be done about that?"

"I want to make people proud of me."

"Then you have to do things that merit their pride."

"That's why I want to be a lawyer."

"You've got to do it because you want to do it. Not for anyone else. You can't care what others think."

"But I do care."

"Seems like we're going in a circle here."

"Let me ask you something, Jim. Am I a burden to you?"

"You've got some issues…"

"I can't believe you said that. How could you say that?"

"What? What'd I say?"

"You call me a case and don't think anything is wrong?"

"I didn't say you were a case."

"You did too. You said I had issues, like something is wrong with me."

"Sara? Do you think you're perfect?"

"I am the VIRGIN MARY. I AM perfect. I'm not a case."

"Wow. That's something I just don't know about."

"I know you don't know. Nobody does. I've been struggling with this for about five years now."

"It's kind of funny you know."

"Funny?!"

"Here you are, the Virgin Mary and nobody knows."

"I'm going to make sure everyone knows. Eventually, everyone will know."

"Sara, do you have a plan?"

"That changes."

"In what way?"

"The people involved shift. People come and go, but I remain who I am."

"The Virgin Mary."

"Oh? You believe me?"

"It's complex. On some level I could see you that way, but I know what your therapist would say. She'd say it's a delusion."

"I just want God near my heart."

"We all want that."

"If I'm not the Virgin Mary then who am I? I'm just some psychotic mixed up girl."

"Is that so bad?"

"Being the Virgin Mary is better, Jim. It's more."

"Even if it's a delusion?"

"I thought you said you could accept it on some level."

"Yes, but I also think either you are or you are not. I see you as Sara McCutcheon."

"And she's a sick little girl. But the Virgin Mary is strong."

"I can see that, but I also think you've got to admit you're mentally ill."

"Why?"

"You have got to play by the rules. Especially if you want to be a lawyer, you've got to learn to play by the rules."

"Let me tell you something. My first hospitalization, the first one, they had me voluntarily sign to be admitted."

"So...?

"If I volunteered that I had a mental illness, then I can un-volunteer myself too."

"I don't think it works that way, Sara."

"Why not?"

"A lot of water has passed under the dam since then. You've been treated for mental illness, how many years? Going on six? You can't just drop off the map and say you're no longer mentally ill. That's how a lot of people know you. Just even mental health court...you got preferential treatment by virtue of your illness. You can't just say you no longer are mentally ill."

"I admit. I was mentally ill, but I've recovered."

"And switched to being the Virgin Mary?"

"Well, yes...sort of."

"That's your illness, Sara. You're trying to be something you aren't. How can you even think you are?"

"Because I take on people's sins."

"What?!

"I take on people's sins so Jesus doesn't have to."

"Oh my God. How do you do that?"

"I do it all in my mind. It's private to me."

"Why would you even want to do that? Are you out of your mind?"

"You already have asked me that."

"When did you start taking on people's sins?"

"When I was with Bain. I wanted us to be forgiven for what we'd done."

"What?"

"I felt so unclean. Then I noticed others did too. I worked to forgive them and see them in a more positive light."

"Do you think people want to be forgiven for their sins? I see most people moving through life without a care."

"Do you really think so?"

"I see most people locked into competition with each other and would be damned if they were going to seek forgiveness for their wrongs."

"I know, Jim."

"You know this?"

"That's why I am having such a tough time."

"You need to get in with some good people."

"That's what I like in you, Jim. You don't compete with others."

"Whoa. What?"

"You don't seem to be too competitive. You're easy going. Easy to talk to."

"With some people I am."

"Not everyone?"

"I'm competitive against Republicans."

"Well who isn't?"

"And I don't go in for the sports heroes everyone is so crazy about."

"How do you compete against that?"

"I don't worship them like most guys do."

"Groovy."

"But in some sense you're right. I'm mostly live and let live."

"And I admire you for that."

"It's not so easy to live and let live sometimes."

"I want to work for the tough-to-love type people."

"What's that?"

"I want to fight for justice among the downtrodden."

"How you going to do that?"

"By loving them."

"You have to have love in your heart to do that you know."

"That's where my boyfriend would come in."

"The last boyfriend you had…that Bain fellow…he wouldn't give you the love you needed."

"The only thing Bain taught me was how to get around rules."

"Again, I'll warn you. If you're a lawyer you'll have to play by the rules."

"I think I can achieve what I want to within the parameters of the law."

"Do you have a plan?"

"I plan to follow in the path that George Fairweather blazed with his Fairweather Lodge Model."

"Ah, yes. I know it well. Peer support among the mentally ill will make them well."

"That's it. That's my dream. To grow Fairweather."

"How big?"

"I don't have any boundaries around that. As big as I can go."

Just then Bill McCutcheon came into the room.

"Couldn't help but overhearing. Sara? You're going to dedicate your life to Fairweather?"

"Essentially, yes. That is my intention."

"Dad," said Jim. "Sara is becoming my hero…heroine."

"I'm proud of you, Sara," said Bill. "You have a mission. Not everyone has one. I don 't believe I started out with one myself. Things just kind of happened. But, hey, you've even met this George Fairweather at a conference, I seem to remember."

"He made a big impression on me. I guess he's my Randall Smith."

"Nice."

"Everyone should have a person they look up to," said Sara.

"I look up to you," said Jim.

"That's corny," smiled Sara.

30

Bill was seeing Ms. Seneca.

"So, my dyspnea means that I could be more susceptible to a heart attack."

"You better get your house in order."

"Do you have to be so cold?"

"Bill, we're both adults. We don't need to pussyfoot around do we, or do we?"

"I'd like a little more compassion from you if that's possible."

"Sure. I can be compassionate, but I want to impress upon you the urgency of coming to terms with Sara and Dorothy."

"Don't you think I know that?"

"I'm sorry. I guess I just see so clearly what you should do, and I'm trying to make you see it too. I just want so much for my patients."

"You think I need to give more of myself, but love is a two-way street. It's very complex. Sara and Dorothy have not exactly been overwhelming with their outpouring of love."

"You're the father and husband. Maybe you have to make the first move."

"And I think I have."

"Well you could start by being nicer to others."

"I am nice."

"Well, you haven't shown that to me. You throw yourself at me and then wonder why I can't fix everything."

"Ms. Seneca…"

"I'll say it again, Bill. It won't do anybody any good for us to pussyfoot around the issue."

"It's not the kind of relationship I've had with Sara and Dorothy, to give everything emotionally to them."

"What then has been the nature of your relationship with them?"

"Civil. Respectful. These are words that come to mind. My highest aspiration is that she would be free."

"Sounds impossible."

"I wanted a life that was elevated above the everyday. I didn't want just another family. I wanted us each to have our individuality. Then when Sara started having problems, then Dorothy left, well, there was a void. Sara and I started going for each other's throat. We had never done that before. Sara had always worked out her problems by herself. But then it was too much for her. She began going down the tubes."

"Was it getting bad?"

"Well, yes. That is what I'm saying."

"Maybe she was seeking release from you. Maybe she had been more dependent on you and Dorothy than you thought. When this Bain character came along, he presented her an opportunity to make a break."

"He may have aided her in wanting freedom, but he couldn't provide it. I just hate to give Bain any credit."

"Bain is insignificant. Could have been anybody. The point is that Sara was ready to make her break from her parents."

"Really."

"It's not so uncommon. Rebellion is very common. People need to shift boundaries from time to time. This is especially true it seems to me in Sara's case."

"I just didn't go in for all the yelling that was a part of it."

"Maybe that was the only way she could handle it. On the one hand, she turned aggressive, but on the other hand, she was passively still recognizing your authority over her. Perhaps she couldn't deal with it in the most adult manner."

"I guess that makes sense. But where does that leave us now?"

"Sara is taking steps now. She is taking huge steps in fact. This lawyer thing, well, it's a huge step for her. Aren't you seeing some changes?"

"I think she's going to need a support system."

Ms. Seneca smiled. "I know where you got yours. One person – Randall Smith."

"Well, Dorothy too."

"Does Sara still have AA or Fairweather?"

"She goes to AA meetings, but she's out of Fairweather for now. They kicked her out for…"

"I know. I heard the story. I don't think she stole the watch though. It was a setup."

"You never know the motives behind people when they target someone, but…"

"Bill, you're naïve. Apparently, the person was jealous of Sara or was threatened by Sara, or…"

"Some people just love to burn someone else just because it makes them feel better. It's called one-up manship."

Ms. Seneca thought back to the time she told Sara they were going to burn Sara's past.

"Sometimes you have to close the door on someone." Ms. Seneca said, but not too enthusiastically.

"I had to close the door on Sara's old boyfriend, that Bain fellow."

"I tried to get Sara to drop him too," said Ms. Seneca while realizing she had told Sara to forget her past even before Ms. Seneca knew about Bain.

"Yes? Is that right?"

"Yeah." Ms. Seneca was telling a white lie to protect herself.

"But Sara's making good decisions now. She's trying to take control of her life. She's trying to forget her past."

Ms. Seneca was relieved she might have had the right instinct in telling Sara to burn her past.

"Yes, I agree. Maybe we should stop for now."

When Bill got home it was just 6:00 in the evening. The lights in the home were on this early November night. He could see Sara and Jim at the computer in his office through the window. Upon entering the home, he found Dorothy cooking in the kitchen.

"Hi, hon'," said Bill.

"Hon'?"

"For the sake of the kids, we have to put up a united front," said Bill.

"You think by calling me hon' we'll save the kids?"

"It's a start."

"Ok hon'"

Sara and Jim came out of the office and into the dining room. They could hear Bill and Dorothy in the kitchen.

"They sound like they're amicable," said Sara.

"Why wouldn't they be?" asked Jim.

"There's so much going on."

"Such as?"

"Where do I start? How about you and me? We're in AA. We're working at part-time jobs to pay a fee that we could earn in a week. We're going back to college, then law school. We're clients in Mental Health Court. We've experienced homelessness. Then about them. Bill's health is going down. Dorothy and he got back together to save us. Bill is in therapy…"

"Hello, kids," said Dorothy coming into the room.

She carried a plate of meatloaf in one hand; potatoes in the other.

"Did you wash your hands?"

"Mom, you treat us like teenagers." Sara chimed in.

"That's because I care about you."

"That's right. I know you care about us, Mom." Jim was being the diplomat.

"It would be nice if you cared about us," said Bill.

"Oh, I do," said Jim.

"How about you, Sara?" Bill raised his gaze towards Sara.

"I'm a little torn apart right now," said Sara.

"Let's sit."

Dorothy was bringing in the remaining dishes. She glanced over at Bill and shrugged her shoulders as if to say, "Who isn't torn apart?"

"Tell me a little more, Sara," said Bill taking a chair.

"I can't talk about it. It's too much."

"Really." Bill was astonished.

"The depths of my heart are too great to be fathomed." Sara looked full of pride.

"Maybe we should put you on a pedestal." Dorothy had to get her two cents in.

"Leave her alone," Jim stepped in.

"I just don't get it," said Bill.

"I'm the Virgin Mary, and I'm trying to save the world by bringing Christ back," said Sara. "It's that simple."

"You're simple all right," said Dorothy.

"Wait now. Whoa," said Bill trying to maintain control. "We can be rational human beings here."

"I don't want to be rational. Christ wasn't rational," said Sara.

Bill realizing Sara had not worked through her rebellion against him took a different tact.

"What's your method in irrationality, Sara?"

"Justice for all."

Sara was really going for the big ideas.

"Now how are you going to do that, Sara?"

Bill thought if he kept questioning her he could get her to stumble.

"You were for that, Bill."

"I was?"

"Yes. At least through your hero, Randall Smith."

"Are you saying you are like Randall Smith?"

"I'm bigger. Bigger than Smith."

"Don't you think you're being a little grandiose?" Dorothy piped in.

"It just is."

"How did you come to this understanding, Sara?" Bill asked.

"God guided me."

"He actually told you you were the Virgin Mary?"

"He did indicate that, yes."

"So how do you live that out?"

"I think I'm doing a pretty good job."

"What are you doing exactly?"

"Loving people."

"How?"

"In my mind."

"You'll have to do a lot more than that if you want to be the Virgin Mary."

"I thought you always taught me that love was the highest value a person could strive for."

"If you think you can love everyone and everyone will love you, then good luck."

"Randall Smith does that."

"OK. I won't argue any more with you, Sara. Your mind is made up. I would just like to know if you have a plan on how you're going to bring this about."

"Become a lawyer."

"Hah! Do you think people love lawyers?"

"People love justice."

"When it goes in their favor."

"Justice doesn't go in anyone's favor. You're a judge? You should know."

"I'm in the dark, Sara. Please enlighten me."

"Justice is when everyone has a sense of home, somebody to talk to, and a fear of God."

"You have it all wrapped up in a nice package, don't you?"

"I think there are parameters that can be attained in the pursuit of justice."

"Oh, so it's a pursuit? You never get there?"

"No. I pursue Jesus's face but never attain it."

Sara looked so somber and at the same time had just a hint of a smile.

"You just approach it. There is no final moment."

"I can see you've thought about this, Sara."

"A lot."

At that, Dorothy jumped in.

"It's getting late. I suggest the two kids go clean their rooms, then call it a night."

Bill couldn't decide if all of Sara's talk of love and justice was just another form of rebellion or if she really believed it.

31

Bill and Sara were at the kitchen table about 9 PM.

"So, Sara, we have covered a lot of ground these past couple of years."

Sara sat back in her chair. "Yes, we have."

"You were quite rebellious against my authority for some time."

"But, I needed…"

"Sara, I know. It wasn't as I would have had it, but you had some testing to do…and some growing which lately you've done."

"So I suppose I owe you an apology for that stuff before."

"I don't know."

"I made some mistakes with you, Dad."

"In the interest of honesty, I will say you did."

Sara's chin dropped.

Bill continued, "But I say this, Sara, because I think you can handle it."

"I can?"

"Most people can't, Sara."

"Can't what?"

"Face the truth. Especially when they've done something they later view as wrong. But you're different from others, Sara."

"Maybe it's because I have you to lean on."

"I know my position as judge and your father give you a point to rally against..."

"But I'm not against you now," Dad.

"But you were for a long time, Sara. I, however, won't stand in judgement against you. You were just being yourself, maybe even your best self."

"Dad, I appreciate your sentiment, but it's not entirely true, especially my relationship with Bain."

"Sara, you know I never liked Bain, but I understand the lure he offered you."

"But, Dad, you never were lured by that in your life."

"I'm not so sure about that, Sara, and that's all I'm going to say about my past. This, now, at this time, is about you."

"Wow."

"Sara, I'm passing you the torch and the McCutcheon name."

"Dad, this is all so formal, and I don't think I deserve such a gift."

"You could call it a gift, but it's more than that. It gives you certain rights."

"Which are?"

"The right to be proud of who you are."

"Isn't pride a sin?"

"It very might well be, at least in God's eyes. But I'm talking about you. I'm giving you the right to be proud."

"You don't think I am already?"

"Sara, I'm sorry, but I don't. You don't have the kind of pride I mean."

"This is all so heavy."

"If you don't think you can handle it..."

"No, Dad. I want what you have."

"Then the kind of pride I talking about is being true to yourself, like Shakespeare said."

"Are you talking about my thing with the Virgin Mary?"

"You could say that."

"But Dad, I hear voices telling me I am."

"Then you need to examine those voices more carefully."

"But they're overwhelming."

"That's why doctors prescribe meds. But meds aren't the whole answer. You have to put in your footwork too."

"Dad, I think you're giving me a mission."

"Yes, I am. Do you accept?"

"I'll do my best."

32

"Oh my God! Sara. Jim."

Dorothy put her hand on Bill's wrist checking for a pulse. She had knocked on Bill's door and not hearing a response, had entered his bedroom, and found him on his bed.

"What Mom? What do you want?" said Sara coming into the room.

It only took a spilt second before she figured out what was going on.

"Is there a heartbeat?" Sara gasped.

"NO." "Call 911".

The funeral was at Memorial Methodist Church. There were some of the lawyers Bill had known, Scott Jensen, Maria Gonzales, Judge Somany, and others, and church people that had known him, and of course, Molly. Dorothy and Sara and Jim sat up front, and Randall Smith sat in back.

Then it was Sara's time to speak.

"Some of you are here to pay your respects to my dad, a judge, a man of caring, and a man who loved his family. I am here as his daughter to say my goodbye. It was all too quick. But that's usually the case in life.

"I remember being his little Sara for my growing up years. Nothing could sever the bond between me and Bill. I call him Bill because that's what he became to me. An equal.

"Abraham Lincoln thought it was obvious that we are equals in life, but it didn't start out that way with me and my dad. I was in awe of him and everything he did astounded me. I put him on a high pedestal and worshipped the ground he walked on.

"He didn't take it that way though. He had his own heroes, and he never thought he would be anyone else's hero. But he was mine...always.

"This is despite what some of you might think, some of you who knew about our tough times whether through the newspaper or otherwise. But I knew...always knew...where he stood in my heart. The sadness I have over his passing is that he may not have known this himself. There were certainly no indications by my behavior around him, what I said and what I did.

"Isn't it strange that I never had a chance? Death grabbed him way before I was ever able to say anything like "I love you" to him.

"Yet, somehow, someway, I think he knew. He knew what a great man I thought he was. I had and still have an illness that makes life a little unpredictable to me and hence my behavior can be surprising to others...except Bill. He always saw me for who I was, his little girl. Sometimes I found that to be stifling, but now I am quite comforted knowing I am still under his wing.

"But there's more to the story. In his last days I saw him begin to let me go. Let me go on with my own life. I don't think I can fathom what this took from him, but I could see him doing it. My dad had a tight hold on my heart so I know how difficult this was, and for me. But I went kicking and screaming all the way. Bill never said, 'Boo'.

"Now it is my turn. My turn to let Bill go. Undoubtedly, he has headed for heaven to be with the saints. I must stay back here on Earth, but not alone. I will always know he watches over me, and for that I am grateful. I am grateful because now in death I realize what he meant in life."

Sara took her place in the pew and smiled a soft smile towards Jim. The church broke into a hymn, then a prayer, and then that was it. A once vibrant life was no more. No more on this Earth, left to the prayers and memories.

"We must keep our good memories," said Dorothy to the kids.

Then there was a gathering in the social hall where food was served and where Sara and Dorothy stood in a greeting line. One of the first ones through the line was Randall Smith.

"Cool. That was really cool what you said, Sara." Smith's smile was tight, but Sara couldn't see his eyes because of his dark glasses.

"Thanks, Randall. Thanks for being here."

Not wishing to draw a crowd, Smith left, disappearing in a limousine.

When the three – Dorothy, Sara, and Jim - got home, they collapsed on the living room furniture. Everyone was a little misty-eyed and not much for words. In the days that had led up to the funeral, they had shared their sorrow. Dorothy had been pleasantly surprised at Sara's maturity. Truth be told, Sara surprised herself too. That night Sara spent most of the night looking at her ceiling and building up her gumption to go on.

She would go to her job at Amazon, and Jim would go to his job with the Washington Lodge, and life would continue. That's what Bill would have wished, and now in death, he was getting his way.

CPSIA information can be obtained
at www.ICGtesting.com
Printed in the USA
FSHW010851050121
77399FS

9 781839 455001